DEATH WISH

For
Charles Pritchard
staunchest of friends
who knows what it's all about

DEATH WISH

STUART JACKMAN

A LION BOOK

Text copyright © 1998 Stuart Jackman

The author asserts the moral right
to be identified as the author of this work

Published by
Lion Publishing
Sandy Lane West, Oxford, England
ISBN 0 7459 3971 6

First edition 1998
10 9 8 7 6 5 4 3 2 1 0   07622650

All rights reserved

A catalogue record for this book is available
from the British Library

Typeset in 13/14.5 Bembo
Printed and bound in Great Britain by
Biddles Ltd, Guildford and King's Lynn

'For me to die is gain.'

Philippians 1:21

PART ONE

1

It was just after 5.30 in the morning when I locked up the house, tossed my bag on to the rear seat of the Lancia coupé and started the engine. I sat for a minute or so letting it warm up and then drove down the hill into Tremezzo, turning south on to the lakeside road for Como.

The first week in April: a hint of frost in the air, the early morning sunlight dazzling on the snow-capped mountains, the lake still in black shadow. It was a moment of great beauty and dark foreboding; a time for remembering things best forgotten.

Ferris had been reticent over the phone the night before. 'A small favour, Mike,' he had said. But it had to be more than that. It always was with Ferris. I listened to the beat of the engine drumming on the walls of the houses as I passed through the little fishing villages. It sounded like a call to arms.

From Como I took the autostrada to Milan. The traffic was minimal and I made good time. The clock on the dashboard read 7.40 when I drew into the long-stay car park at Linate Airport.

'Colonel Lucas?' The girl on the Al Italia desk had my ticket ready. 'Just the one bag, sir?'

I nodded. 'A couple of days,' Ferris had said. 'Three at the most. And come in uniform, Mike.' Which meant he didn't want me to be seen dropping into his office in civvies as if I were still on his payroll. Watching eyes, noting the caducei badges on my lapels, would lose interest. As they had so often in the past. Nobody suspects a doctor.

The girl gave me my boarding pass. 'There you go, sir. Enjoy the flight.' She smiled as if she meant it.

I went through into the departure lounge for coffee and a panino before take-off. Forty minutes later I was in Rome.

Ferris had laid on a car and driver to meet me. A young, starched corporal with big-knuckled hands and a carefully neutral face below the peak of his service cap. I settled into the back seat while he put my bag in the boot. It was nearly four years since I had been in the capital and I had forgotten what the traffic was like. Four quiet years in retirement in a converted farmhouse above Tremezzo with my boat and my trout rods, my ski kit and my memories, working sporadically on a book nobody would dare to publish. A peaceful retreat I had never expected to leave. Watching the seething streets glide past now it seemed unreal. A dream.

Fortunately the corporal knew all the back-doubles and deposited me outside the office block in the Via Flavia with a few minutes to spare before my appointment. The brass plate beside the main entrance, worn smooth with much polishing, still read: EASTERN ISLANDS TRADING COMPANY. An innocent title for activities which were anything but that.

Ferris's secretary greeted me with a smile. 'Quite like old times, Colonel, though you don't look a day older.' She was perhaps forty-five, well-groomed and efficient with a composure not even the brigadier's rasping impatience could ruffle. And when she smiled she was maturely beautiful in a grey-eyed, dark-haired way.

'I'll not see fifty-four again,' I said, touching the grey hair at my temples.

10

'But very fit.'

I grinned. 'That's the skiing, Marcia.' I patted my stomach. 'This will betray me come the summer.' And thought: Ferris permitting.

'Not married yet?' she said, tactfully surprised.

'Not my scene.' I had always been a loner in a trade not conducive to a stable marriage. I enjoy the company of pretty women and have had my moments of passion but liking has never grown to loving.

'Such a waste.' Marcia picked up the house phone, spoke briefly, coloured a little and replaced the receiver. 'The Brigadier says you are to put me down at once and go right in.'

'Chance'd be a fine thing,' I said. 'How is the old tyrant?'

She raised her eyebrows in mock disapproval. 'That's for you to decide. You're the doctor.'

'Touché,' I said. My father had been a Greek physician with a Roman wife (herself a Ward Sister) and I had followed him into the profession, joining the Imperial Army Medical Corps on qualifying, serving as a regimental MO in Spain and North Africa before specializing in psychiatric medicine to research the problems of battle fatigue in troops stationed in the troubled provinces of the Eastern Mediterranean. A roving commission which had taken me to military hospitals from Damascus and the Lebanon, through Israel and Egypt into Turkey and the Balkans. It was the ideal cover for a field agent and back in 42 Ferris had co-opted me into CI2 to target suspected subversives involved in a variety of covert operations against the Pax Romana.

Ferris came out from behind his desk as I entered. A

bulky, grizzled old warrior with a blunt chin, ice-blue eyes and the restless energy of a thirty-year-old in his ageing body. He was an ex-cavalry officer who had been persuaded some twenty years previously to leave his beloved tanks and take command of CI2 – Counter Intelligence, Eastern Mediterranean section. 'Mike. Good of you to come.' He gripped my hand hard.

I smiled wryly. 'Did I have a choice?'

He grinned, showing white, even teeth, indicated a chair and sat down opposite me, spruce as ever in a dark suit, striped shirt, bold bow tie, his shoes like black mirrors. 'You're looking very chipper. Retirement obviously suits you.'

'Enough not to relish being reactivated.'

'Hardly that. You'll be back in Tremezzo the day after tomorrow. You can bank on that.'

But what happens tomorrow? I thought.

Marcia came in with coffee. 'Black, no sugar, Colonel. Right?' She had an extraordinary memory for detail; which was why Ferris employed her.

'No phone calls. No visitors,' he growled. 'Clear?'

'No need to throw your weight about either,' she said sweetly. 'I do know the drill. Sir.'

Watching their faces, sensing the rapport between them, I wondered – not for the first time – if they were secretly married. And rather hoped they were.

When she had left us, I said, 'What's on the agenda?'

Ferris spooned sugar recklessly into his coffee, tasted it and said, 'I need a doctor. Not for myself. For an old patient of yours.'

'Oh yes? Who?'

'Troax.' The rasp in his voice was like the scrape of a match to light a fuse.

'Ah.' I had spent a lot of time on Paul Troax, the self-appointed leader of ICHTHUS – a secret society, ostensibly religious but with political undertones. Founded back in the 30s in Jerusalem as a Jewish sect it had, under his dynamic leadership, spread through Turkey into Greece and the Balkans with a tenuous foothold in Rome itself. An orthodox Jew from Tarsus in South Turkey, he was also a free-born Roman citizen. A man living in two worlds, accepted by neither. Suspected by his own kind, who branded him as a dangerous heretic, despised by the Romans and Greeks, who saw him as a ghetto brat on the make, he had been my main target and had, over the years, become my friend. A fact which I had been careful to conceal from Ferris. 'He's still alive, is he?'

Ferris nodded. 'And still where you left him four years ago. Under house arrest here in Rome.'

'And he's ill?' I said, unsurprised. Cage a tiger for four years and you sap his strength, paralyze his mind.

'No. Old and frail, as you'd expect, but not ill. You're here wearing your CI2 hat, Mike, not your doctor's.'

'I thought his file was closed?' I said, not much liking the sound of this.

'Not closed. Shelved, perhaps, but still active. He sits in his garret writing letters, briefing his agents. Like a spider in its web. And it's a very big web now and growing by the month.'

'He's a deeply religious man, y'know,' I said, but not apologetically. Nobody apologized for Troax. Feared him, abused him, loved him but never apologized for him. As well apologize for a hawk stooping on its prey.

'Oh, he's deep all right. Whether or not it's religious depth's another matter.' Ferris scowled. Like most

Romans of his class he had little time for religion, paying lip service to the old gods of Olympus in who he no longer believed. He swallowed a mouthful of coffee, grimaced and added yet more sugar. 'D'you hear much news up there in your mountain hideaway?'

'Only what comes on the box.' Which, under the draconian censorship laws Nero had forced through the Senate, was neither informative nor reliable.

'Nero-speak,' Ferris said contemptuously. 'That megalomaniac'll be the death of Rome yet. If he has his way Troax'll end up with the lions in the Colosseum.'

'He doesn't deserve that,' I said quickly.

'Perhaps not. More to the point, we can't afford it.' Those cold blue eyes met mine with a kind of wounded anger. 'Rome's sick, Mike. Bankrupt of money, of morality too. Fraud. Slander. Corruption in the law courts, sleaze in the Senate, oppression in the streets and a raving lunatic on the throne.'

I shrugged. 'Politics always was a dirty game.'

'It's not just politics – or what passes for politics in that talking-shop in the Forum. The disease has spread to the armed forces. Morale is at an all-time low. The troops unpaid and mutinous, their officers buffoons posturing under the patronage of Nero, vulgar in the mess, a disaster in the field.'

'That bad?' I said, appalled. The Empire was sustained by its military muscle. If that went flaccid...

'You'd better believe it, Mike. We're sitting on a time-bomb here and the fuse is lit and burning fast. Nero's close to panic and looking for a scapegoat to divert the hatred of the plebs. The word is he'll go for the Christians this time, as he went for the Jews before.'

I had heard the title *Christian* first some twenty-odd

years ago in Antioch; the followers of Jesus Davidson, called the Christ, whose symbol was a fish. It had been an insult then, coined by the Jews in the ghettos of Turkey. A sneering jibe hurled at a handful of their own kind who had defected to the Davidson cult. A jibe Troax had turned into a title of honour as the sign of the fish began to appear scrawled on walls as far away as Greece.

'Nero's planning to present them as the source of all our troubles,' Ferris said. 'And Troax as an enemy of the people. A set-piece show trial on TV, he himself the judge and jury. Prosecuting counsel too probably – you know how he likes to hog the cameras – with a carefully rehearsed and bribed rabble of witnesses mouthing their lies on cue. A prime-time programme on all channels, the verdict decided before it begins. And the next day, an agonizing death on the sand below the terraces. Without dignity, without mercy.'

I shook my head. 'The Senate won't wear that. Troax is a Roman citizen and...'

'The Senate will do as it's told. Spineless yes-men who owe their seats to Nero.' Ferris leaned forward in his chair, shoulders hunched, fists clenched on his thighs. 'Remember how he let the mob loose on the Jews? The carnage in the streets, the butchery, the burning? If Troax goes to the lions it'll be the Christians' turn, massacred to keep that madman on his throne. Are we to stand idly by and watch him tear the heart out of Rome – out of the Empire? I think not.'

'We?' I said.

He sat back, his anger under control. 'There are still a few of us left, Mike. Loyal to the old laws that made Rome great. Half-a-dozen military chiefs, including the

CO of the Praetorian Guard. Hallam, the Home Secretary. Vince, the Minister of Defence. Men of courage and probity prepared to stand up and be counted. We've been putting our heads together to find a way to defuse this crisis.'

'Ah,' I said. 'A political solution, is it?'

'Of course.' He looked surprised. 'It's always been political. What else?'

'Religious. A question of belief, not of politics.'

He shrugged. 'Either way it's critical so long as Troax lives.'

'You're not suggesting a mercy killing, are you? Because if that's why you've sent for me, forget it.'

'Easy, Mike. I wouldn't pull you back for that. No, we're going to smuggle him out of Rome quietly, without fuss.'

I shook my head. 'He won't go. He's set his heart on a trial here. Worked for it. Risked his life for it. He won't let you rescue him now.'

'That's why we need you, Mike. To persuade him to see sense.'

'Why me?'

'Because he trusts you,' Ferris said simply. And told me the plan.

It was a good plan. Logical, daring. And I said as much. 'But even if he agrees to all that – and it's a big If – what're you going to tell Nero?'

'That his prisoner has unfortunately died. The certificate specifying a massive heart attack has already been prepared and lacks only the signature of a doctor. The guards on the house where he is being held will bear witness to his death. Nero has never seen Troax. A substitute corpse now in the mortuary in the military hospital will be available to satisfy his morbid curiosity. And that will be that. He'll hit the roof, of course. Cheated of his prey, his grand strategy in ruins. But we can handle that. A small price to pay to save Rome from destruction.'

He made it sound easy, foolproof. But I knew how many things could go wrong with Nero's spies seeded in the streets.

'I know what you're thinking,' Ferris said. 'But what's the alternative? Death to the Christians. Innocent people massacred. The city set alight. Total breakdown of law and order. Is that what you want?'

'It might not come to that,' I said, knowing it would. Troax would go into the arena as a Christian Jew, doubly damned in the eyes of the mob.

'That's a risk we daren't take, I'm afraid,' Ferris said sombrely.

We sat in silence for a moment or two. I was dully aware of the traffic noise in the street below, of the little coloured stars on the map covering the wall opposite Ferris's desk, each one representing a field agent. Four years ago I had been one of them; a star travelling west across the Mediterranean, bringing Troax on his final voyage to what he was convinced would be his crowning triumph in the heart of the Empire. 'I suppose you want me to sign the death certificate?' I said then.

'Yes.'

'Why me? There's no shortage of army medics in GHQ.'

'And find themselves facing a court martial for failing to keep Troax alive? Going to the lions in his place?'

'Thank you for those cheerful words.'

Ferris grinned. 'You will not sign your own name,

obviously. You're now an unfamiliar face in Rome, no longer associated with CI2. Above suspicion. And by the time Nero sees the certificate you'll be back in Tremezzo. Out of sight, out of mind.' He saw the doubt in my eyes. 'Don't worry about it, Mike. We've got it all buttoned up.'

'So why bring me down here to scrawl a false name on a piece of paper?'

'Ah, well,' he said. 'There's rather more to it than that. The plan to rescue Troax relies for its success – initially at least – on your relationship with him.'

I looked at him bleakly, aware of the devious mind behind his smile. 'You haven't told me the whole story, have you?'

'Not quite, no.'

'Then I think it's time you did,' I said. 'Sir.'

'Of course,' he said equably. 'I was coming to that.'

2

He was waiting for me in the ante-room of the GHQ mess when I came out after lunch.

'Colonel Lucas?' He was young and lean in combat denims, captain's pips on his shoulders, the gold flash of the Praetorian Guard on his sleeves. Black hair cut short in the military fashion, a face older than his years. I saw the blue-on-red ribbon of the Imperial Star on his chest taking pride of place over a row of campaign medals. That said it all. 'Reynaud, sir. Piers Reynaud.' He spoke with a Toulon accent and that said something too. Not many Frenchmen made it to the elite Praetorians. An exceptional soldier, then, hand-picked by Ferris for sure. 'My chaps will be providing the muscle tomorrow – if necessary.'

I nodded, liking him. 'You know what's involved?'

'I've been briefed, sir, yes.' His voice was carefully neutral. 'I've got transport laid on. I understand you want to talk to the prisoner this afternoon?'

'Yes.' What Ferris had called softening him up and I called preparing him.

'When you're ready then, sir.'

The jeep was parked outside. Two men in the rear seats. Big men. Armed. Reynaud saw me looking at their automatic rifles. 'Just showing the flag, sir. Things are a bit fraught just now.'

'Very sensible.'

The afternoon was fine and mild, the city looking its magnificent best. A day for sitting in the sun outside a trattoria, drinking wine with a girl; for music and laughter and falling in love. Or for betraying the trust of a friend to save his life.

We drove across town past the Forum and the big banking houses and the smart shops. The pavements were busy with well-dressed men and elegant women, citizens of the world's greatest city, the glittering hub in the wheel of the Empire.

'You can almost smell the money, can't you?' Reynaud said wryly, driving the jeep with effortless skill through the traffic.

Outside the Colosseum a group of tourists stood listening to the guide, cameras at the ready. Smell the blood too, I thought. And was oddly comforted. At least we were saving him from that.

We swung left over the bridge across the Tiber and were suddenly in a different world of mean streets choked with litter, flies and filth and the stench of the fishmarket. This was a Rome tourists never saw. Open sewers instead of ornamental fountains, crumbling tenements instead of marble villas, ragged children, slatternly women, junkies, winos, muggers who would maim a man for the price of a fix. The slum at the journey's end of a man born in a Turkish ghetto who had spoken in kings' houses, addressed the Athenian intelligentsia in the Areopagus and become a household name in a score of cities around the Eastern Mediterranean, feared by the civic authorities, reviled by the trades unions, hunted by the police. But among his own respected, revered, loved. A man now returned to squalor and poverty, his wings clipped, his voice muted, all the glory departed. In my end is my beginning.

The house was at the end of an alley. A three-storied ruin held up by its neighbours, the ground-floor windows boarded up, anti-Semitic filth scrawled across the battered door. A Redcap corporal was standing outside looking bored; a polished and blancoed alien in the verminous underworld. He snapped to attention, saluting as we drove up.

'Where is he?' I said to Reynaud.

'Top floor, sir. D'you want me to come up?'

'I'll manage, thanks.'

He looked doubtful. I suppose to him I was an old man past my prime. 'Are you sure? The Provost Marshal says Troax can be a bit of a handful when the mood takes him. Regular little firebrand, surprisingly stroppy for his size.'

I smiled, remembering. 'He won't give me any trouble, Reynaud.'

'If you say so, sir. There's another Redcap on the landing outside his room if...'

'No problems then.'

He grinned. 'We'll come back at 18.00 hours if that suits?'

I nodded and went inside.

The soldier on the landing checked my pass signed by Ferris, unlocked the door, stood aside to let me in and locked it behind me.

The room was small with a dormer window let into the sloping ceiling. Bare floorboards ingrained with dirt, a truckle bed, a couple of orange boxes stuffed with paperbacks, a kitchen chair, a chipped enamel washbowl on an iron stand. The whole place exuded the sickly-sweet smell of the bugs infesting the plastered walls. Troax had known better rooms – and many worse ones.

He was sitting on the bed, a biro in his hand, a pad of cheap notepaper on his knee. He was wearing a woollen shirt and faded jeans, his body shrunken and frail, his once black hair white now and sparse. His left eye was half-closed, the lashes sticky with mucus, and his face was withered, the skin like parchment. I had forgotten how small he was and how ugly. But when he looked up and smiled, his good eye welcoming, the years telescoped and I was back in Damascus where it had all begun, doing Philip Marron, our consul there, a favour.

'I wouldn't ask, old boy,' Marron said apologetically; a plump, urbane man on his way up the diplomatic ladder, relaxed and easy with a fellow Roman, 'only Rabbi Kohbar's a good sort. Very co-operative. He's persuaded his congregation to accept our presence here with good grace. Makes my job easier all round.'

I smiled cautiously. 'I get the message. You scratch each other's backs. So what's the bottom line?'

'He's been having a spot of bother with this Davidson cult. They're heretics, d'you see? Naughty boys. They've been making waves and he doesn't like it much. Religious waves.' He shook his head. 'Very dodgy.'

'Really?' I said patiently. Marron was not known for coming to the point. Few diplomats are.

'You'd better believe it, Mike. Anyway, Kohbar phoned an SOS call to Jerusalem last week asking for Saul Troax. He's the laddie in charge of the High Priest's anti-heresy unit. Hot stuff, too, from all I hear. They say he's really put the frighteners on Davidson's followers down there. Mass arrests, interrogations, durance vile – the full treatment. A sort of pogrom by the Jews. Quirky, eh?'

'Different, anyway.'

'Absolutely. So this Troax character floats in here

yesterday with a squad of heavies from the Temple Guard, all set to clean up the town. Only...'

'Only what?' I said a touch impatiently now. Once Marron got the bit between his teeth there was no stopping him.

'Something happened on the way up here. One of these freak storms we get at this time of the year north of Galilee caught them out in the open and Troax's car was struck by lightning – or something similar.'

'Ah,' I said, recognizing my cue. 'He needs a doctor, does he? Is he badly burned?'

'You'd expect that, wouldn't you? But no. Not a mark on him apparently. But it blinded him. He's in Kohbar's house in Straight Street now, helpless as a child.'

'Sorry, Phil. I'm a psychiatrist, not an ophthalmic surgeon.'

'My point exactly, old boy. The eye specialist in our local hospital's been in to look at him and says there's no actual physical damage to the eyes. He reckons it's a severe trauma brought on by shock. Mental, d'you see?' Marron tilted his head. 'Your field, I fancy?'

'Well, yes. But I'm booked on the three o'clock flight to Egypt. Due at No. 6 Field Hospital, Heliopolis, this evening.'

'If you could just take a quick look at him? You'll be doing me a big favour. Lots of Brownie points with Kohbar.'

I said I didn't imagine I could do anything in one brief visit but he wasn't listening.

'I've laid on a car. Take you to the airport afterwards. Can do?' He shook my hand enthusiastically. 'Thanks, old boy. I knew I could rely on you.'

Kohbar was a study in black and grey. Black suit, black

hat (worn indoors in the Jewish fashion), long grey beard. A big man with a presence but his welcoming smile was uncertain. I was in uniform and he was not accustomed to entertaining Roman officers in his house. Nor to having a car with CD plates parked outside.

'Thank you for coming, Doctor,' he said with grave courtesy. 'He's in the back room.'

'It's Saul, I believe?' A patient's name is the key to his confidence. Important to get it right. 'What does that mean in Hebrew?'

'"I Asked For."' Kohbar smiled. 'He's an only son and came late in the marriage.' He hesitated. 'He's also a free-born Roman.'

'Ah,' I said, clutching at straws. The more I knew about his background the greater my chance of getting through to him. 'Let's go and have a look at him, shall we?'

The back room was shadowed, the shutters half-closed against the sun. Troax was sitting in a chair, his chin on his chest, his hands slack in his lap. Even in the gloom I couldn't help noticing his clothes – and with some surprise. His suit was expensive, his shirt silk. There were gold links in his cuffs, a gold Rolex Oyster on his wrist, hand-lasted shoes on his feet. A peacock against Kohbar's crow.

The rabbi made to open the shutters.

'No,' I said. 'Leave them as they are for the moment. Shalom, Saul.'

He made no answer; a man sunk inside himself, alone in his misery. I put my hand under his chin and lifted his head. He was astonishingly ugly. Black hairs sprouting out of ears and nostrils, big hooked nose, wide mouth, heavy black brows. He was clean-shaven in the Roman fashion, his skin pitted and sallow. His eyes were his saving feature; clear, large, gypsy-black – and totally blank. There was no reaction when I shone my torch in them.

'Who are you, sir?' His voice was brittle but calm. An outward calm to hide a mind in turmoil. Behind those dark, unfocused eyes was a very frightened man.

I told him my name.

'A Greek?'

'Yes. Serving in the Roman army. The Medical Corps.'

'I am a Roman by birth,' he said with a flash of spirit. 'Does that surprise you?'

'Nothing surprises me, Saul. Nightmares, hallucinations – these are my stock in trade.'

'I'm not imagining this,' he said sharply. 'I really can't see.'

I heard the controlled temper in his voice, the injured pride, the impatience with illness. He had all the makings of a difficult patient. But there was something about him which intrigued me. A kind of truculent arrogance you sometimes find in small, ill-favoured men. And something else. The angry despair of a man of faith whose faith has failed him. 'I know,' I said. 'What was the last thing you saw? Can you remember?'

And again that flash of spirit. 'How could I forget? I saw the Shekinah, heard the voice of God calling my name. That's why I'm blind. I looked at God's face. No man can do that and...'

'Easy, Saul. Just try to relax.'

'You don't believe me, do you? You think I'm mad.' And now there was pleading in his anger; for reassurance, for hope.

'I believe you believe it,' I said carefully. 'Truth has many forms, many names. You're obviously a religious man and find the truth in your faith.'

'Words,' he said bitterly. 'You Greeks are all the same. You talk about truth but know nothing of it.'

'We all do that, Saul. Greeks, Romans – even Jews. We all try to describe the indescribable. You say God called you by name. What else did he say?'

He turned his head impatiently. 'Are you there, Kohbar?'

'I'm here, Saul.'

'Get this ignorant word-spinner out of here. I'm tired of his questions.'

'He's a highly qualified doctor,' Kohbar said unhappily.

'He's wasting his time and mine,' Troax said. 'When God takes away a man's sight only God can restore it.' His head turned blindly to me. 'Leave me in peace, can't you?'

But if ever a man was not at peace with himself, that man was Saul Troax.

Outside in the hall, I said, 'Shekinah?'

Kohbar shrugged, that eloquent raising of the shoulders, part apology, part defiance, the Jews do so well. 'It's our name for the glory of God. The unearthly light in which he moves and has his being. Moses saw it on Sinai, Isaiah in the Temple, Ezekiel in the sky. All the great prophets, the visionaries.'

'Ah,' I said. God in the lightning, his voice in the thunder. 'And what did God say to him?'

'I don't know. He won't talk about it. Gets very uptight if pressed.'

'He's a frightened man, Rabbi. Underneath the bitterness he's really scared.'

'Is that why he's blind?'

'Perhaps. Shock plays strange tricks on the mind. Makes cowards of the bravest of men.' I had seen it so often in hard-bitten veterans emerging from one battle too many, broken in spirit, weeping like children.

'Can you do anything for him, Doctor?'

'Not until he's prepared to talk about it. I'm sorry. It's really a question of time. If I could have him hospitalized, win his confidence, do a little probing...' Sedated, with a strobe light focused on his eyes, a tape-recorder playing a muffled voice against a background of thunder, he might begin to respond.

'We'd willingly meet the cost,' Kohbar said.

I shook my head. 'It's not a problem money can solve. Only time can do that. Unfortunately I'm leaving Damascus this afternoon.'

Kohbar smiled thinly. 'Wait and see, then?' A typically Jewish comment. Humour with just a touch of the macabre. How long would Troax have to wait to see again?

'Something like that.' I saw the disappointment in his face. 'I'm sorry.'

There was a loud knocking on the door. Kohbar frowned, excused himself and opened it. An elderly Jew stood on the step, bearded, shabby in the inevitable long black coat and wide-brimmed hat.

'Ananias,' Kohbar said without warmth. 'What brings you to my house?'

The old man cleared his throat. 'I am sent by God to minister to Saul Troax,' he said hoarsely, fear in his eyes, in his voice, in the nervous clasping and unclasping of his hands.

'My God or yours?' Kohbar's voice was a cold as a stone and as hard.

'Surely they are the same, Rabbi? God is one, so the prophets tell us. The creator and father of us all.'

I thought it a good answer, putting the ball neatly back in Kohbar's court. But the rabbi's response was chilling. 'Wait,' he said and closed the door in Ananias' face.

I raised my eyebrows at such discourtesy. 'One of your congregation?'

'No longer. His kind are not welcome in my synagogue.'

'His kind?'

'He's a heretic and a blasphemer. A follower of Jesus Davidson, the Nazarene carpenter. I'm amazed he has the effrontery to come here at all.'

Having heard something of Troax's reputation I was inclined to agree. Small wonder the old man was afraid. 'He says he's been sent by...'

'He says,' Kohbar said scornfully.

I said, 'Look, Rabbi, the religious niceties are beyond me. But Troax needs help.'

'And you think that – that apostate can help him?'

'I don't know. Sometimes a layman can get through where we professionals fail. He's obviously had to screw up his courage to come here. I'm told Troax has a rough way with Davidson's people. If Ananias is willing to take the risk I think you should give him the chance.'

'I have my position to think of, Doctor. We're a close-knit community here. Misunderstood, vulnerable to gossip. If it became known that I...' He shook his head in self-disgust. 'I'm sorry. You're quite right. We hold a man's future in our hands.' He went back to the door and opened it wide. 'Come in, friend, and may God be with you.'

As we re-entered the room Troax turned his head towards us. I saw the shine of tears in those sightless eyes, the ducts working hard to cleanse the eyeballs. An automatic reflex but, in the circumstances, a useless one. 'Who's there?' he said querulously.

Ananias stepped forward suddenly confident, taking charge as if by right. He knelt beside Troax, put a hand on his shoulder and said, 'Close your eyes.' As Troax's eyelids closed, Ananias touched them gently, smoothing away the tears with his finger. 'Brother Saul,' he said in a strangely disembodied voice which seemed to come from a great distance and sent a shiver down my spine, 'the Lord Jesus who appeared to you on the road has sent me that you may regain your sight and be filled with his spirit.'

'No,' Kohbar said outraged. 'I will not have that name spoken in my house. You go too far, Ananias, and I forbid...' His voice tailed away in awe as Troax opened his eyes cautiously, blinked and said, 'Why aren't the shutters open?'

Ananias stood up, walked to the window and threw the shutters wide. Sunlight flooded into the room; a warm, bright, life-giving tide. And Troax was on his feet, his head held high, his eyes alive and full of wonder. A small, defiant figure touched with radiance, a kind of glory, of vibrant peace. 'Thanks be to God and to his son, Jesus.' His voice thrilled with power. 'Jesus whom I have cruelly persecuted and who this day has called me into his service...'

'Michael Lucas. Is it really you, old friend?' It was the same powerful voice which had made that declaration of faith and loyalty in Damascus all those years ago. The voice of a born street-orator who had blazed a trail of freedom and hope round the eastern Mediterranean, across the Aegean and the Adriatic to Rome itself. A persistent, argumentative voice bringing courage and life to the common people and fear to those set in authority over them. A voice ageless and unimpaired in marked contrast to his ravaged face, emaciated body, thin, old man's hair.

He put his writing pad aside and stood up stiffly, gripping my hand in both of his, the long, arthritic fingers closing like a vice.

'Shalom, Paul.' The greeting stuck in my throat as I remembered why I was there.

'Shalom, shalom, Michael.'

I had always been Michael to him. The soldier angel. We stood grinning at each other, moved beyond words by shared memories. Then we sat down, he on the bed, I on the rickety chair.

'You didn't get that eye fixed, then?' I said.

'No.' He dabbed at his left eye with a threadbare handkerchief; a reflex gesture I remembered so well. He had picked up an infection in a fly-blown village back in the late Forties. I had wanted him to get it treated but he had refused. Too busy, as always, to acknowledge illness. Battling on – diseased eye, malaria, hepatitis, arthritis and all. 'It's not a problem,' he said with a broken-toothed smile. 'I'm used to it now.'

As you are used to those teeth broken by a jailer's mailed fist, I thought. And the shackle scars on your wrists and ankles, the livid, ridged weals under your shirt. 'Are they feeding you properly?'

'Well enough.' Food had never interested him. Nor money, nor creature comforts. His whole being was focused on the faith he was committed to share with all. Since Damascus that had been his life, his reason for living.

Before that it had been different. A well-educated young man, fluent in three languages, he had been the sales manager in his father's textile factory in Tarsus, prospering on lucrative contracts to make tents for the army. He had dressed the part too. The clothes of a gentleman on the squat, ill-favoured body of a ghetto parvenu. In those days he had been an orthodox Jew with ambitions to the rabbinate. Not that there had ever been the slightest chance of that. He had written many times from Tarsus to the High Priest in Jerusalem asking for his name to be brought before the Sanhedrin as a rabbinical candidate. He had all the intellectual qualifications, all the fervour. But the closed shop of the Sanhedrin would never have welcomed a Roman citizen into its company. He had begun to despair when Caiaphas had summoned him to Jerusalem in the Thirties to take charge of the anti-heresy squad briefed to stamp out the Davidson cult. It had been his big break and he had seized it with fanatical zeal. A reign of terror, all the more bitter for being religious, which had come to an abrupt end in Kohbar's house when Saul, the scourge of Davidson's followers, had become Paul, their fiery champion.

Paul. A Roman name meaning 'little'. The personality of a giant in the body of a little man...

'How?' Marron said when I reported back to him that day en route for the Damascus airport. 'How did he do that?'

I shook my head. 'I don't know.' Perhaps it had been lucky timing. The initial shock wearing off, the link between eyes and brain restored. It was unlikely but the only logical explanation. So why was I so reluctant to accept it?

'Hmm,' Marron said. 'And now he's changed sides, has he? Caiaphas'll go spare when he hears.'

'I shouldn't think Davidson's lot'll be too enthusiastic either,' I said. 'Although Ananias is obviously over the moon about it.'

'Yes, well he would be, wouldn't he?' Marron shook his head. 'It's men like Johnson Troax'll have a hard time convincing.'

'Johnson?'

'Peter Johnson. He's running the show now, apparently. Great ox of a man, all fire and thunder. Galilean fisherman. Illiterate, of course. They mostly are, I gather, the original Davidson team. An unlikely bunch to found a new religion. Not an educated man among 'em except John Zebedee. He's a cut above the rest. Bit of a dreamer. Clever with words. Writes Greek poetry, would you believe?'

Johnson. Zebedee. The names meant nothing to me. 'You're really plugged-in to this Davidson thing, aren't you?'

Marron shrugged. 'Part of my job, old boy. Ear to the ground and all that. Defending the dear old Pax Romana. Not that I think they're any kind of a threat to us. It's just one of those domestic religious squabbles the Jews are so fond of.'

'Caiaphas seems worried about them.'

'Yes. Very status-conscious, His Reverence. Has to be with that ditherer Pilate relying on him to run the province. But they seem harmless enough to me. Cranky, of course, but harmless. A few more years and they'll be history. Forgotten.' He grinned impishly. 'But I'll tell you this for free, old son. If Troax goes back to Jerusalem wearing his new Davidson hat there'll be fireworks. My word, yes. There's just not room in that town for him and Johnson...'

'Do they let you have many visitors?' I said now, shifting uncomfortably on the chair.

'Some.' Troax smiled. 'The women are very good to me. Do my laundry, post my letters, bring me books – that sort of thing.'

I looked at his threadbare clothes, the patched cloak spread out on the bed. That was the nearest he'd ever got to a rabbi's gown, that cloak; every mended tear a souvenir of mob violence in so many towns where he'd been manhandled into jail. Compared with the cells he'd been chained up in, this mean little garret was a palace. Until I remembered his former sartorial elegance, the up-market apartment he had occupied in the Temple precinct as Caiaphas' right-hand man. 'And the men?' I said. 'Do they come to see you?'

'Not often. It's too dangerous. The redcaps turn a blind eye to the women but they're suspicious of men.'

'What about the eleven?' The disciples chosen by Davidson from the beginning in Galilee. 'Do you ever see any of them?'

He shook his head. 'They're scattered now. Thomas went to India, y'know. Always the loner but pure gold under that dogged exterior. John Zebedee's in Patmos writing his memoirs. James is still in Jerusalem, quietly diplomatic as ever. I gather he's made us quite respectable there now.' He sounded dubious, as if a respectable Christian was a contradiction in terms.

'So where's Peter Johnson now?' Not in Jerusalem, obviously. Respectability was not his line.

'He's here in Rome. Just the same. Larger than life, impetuous as ever.'

'You've seen him, have you?'

Troax grinned. 'Not *that* impetuous. He had to keep his head down. Under protest, I might add.'

Just as well, I thought, if he wants to keep it on his shoulders. A man without fear, or tact. Brave as a lion, gauche as a teenager.

'He's my heir apparent, of course. When the time comes he'll take over here.' He smiled a little ruefully. 'We've had our differences, Peter and I. He was very wary of me to begin with.'

'With good reason,' I said, answering his smile.

'Oh, quite. He didn't know what to make of me. A vulture turned dove.'

Or eagle, I thought. There was little of the dove in Troax.

'But once he'd got it into his head that we're a world faith, not just a Jewish sect confined to Israel, he backed me to the hilt. I couldn't wish for a better man to hand over the reins to.'

I winced inwardly, knowing how soon that handover would be, all Ferris's logical arguments suddenly flawed in my mind.

'So,' he said, 'what about you, Michael? Where are you living now?'

I told him with an ache in my heart, picturing for him my house above the lake in the peace of the mountains, untouched by the political chicanery of Rome. I spoke of the little fishing villages, the ever-changing moods of the lake, the feeling of space.

'I'm glad for you,' he said, genuinely pleased. 'It sounds marvellous. A foretaste of the Kingdom.'

Hearing the wistfulness in his voice, I felt the room close round us like a cage and was ashamed. The enormity of what I had been brought to Rome to do filled me with self-loathing. We had travelled too long and too far together for it all to end in betrayal.

'So what brings you to Rome?' he said. 'A medical conference?'

'Something like that,' I said lamely.

He nodded. 'Doctors and preachers never retire.' He put a hand on his writing pad. 'I still keep in touch with my churches, you see.'

'Yes.'

'We had some good times, Michael,' he said then.

'And some hard ones.' But I had not shared the hardship, protected by my uniform and profession. The brunt of it all had fallen on his narrow shoulders – the floggings, the stonings, the rat-infested cells – and had, in a curious way, enhanced his stature. Experiences which would have broken physically bigger men had served only to build him up, make him stronger.

He nodded. 'But exciting, eh? Fulfilling. Sharing our Master's suffering, sustained by his power and grace. Like that time in Cyprus. D'you remember?'

3

In the early summer of 42 I flew into Cyprus to sign the discharge papers (with a strong recommendation for a Class A invalidity pension) for a sergeant in the Fifth Legion. The sole survivor when his patrol had been attacked by Bedouin in the Libyan desert, he had been cruelly tortured, losing an eye and one hand and left for dead. When the search-and-rescue chopper had found him he had been out of his mind.

'Lucky to be alive,' the sister of the psychiatric ward said.

Alive, I thought, but hardly lucky.

The military hospital in Paphos commanded a view of the harbour and the sea beyond; a bright, clean, restful place in tree-shaded gardens. It was all lost on the sergeant. He sat in a wheelchair beside his bed, outwardly passive, inwardly haunted by horror. Physically he was healing. Mentally he was beyond our reach. A tough, brave man with an exemplary record reduced to a vacant, dribbling wreck. Better by far if he had died.

I was in the sister's office making arrangements to have him flown home when the phone rang.

'It's for you, sir,' the sister said. 'General Paulus.'

Sergius Paulus was the Military Governor; a thickset, straight-down-the-line veteran who ran the island like a gunnery school, was a stickler for protocol, transparently honest and surprisingly popular with the locals.

'Heard you were on my patch, Lucas.' The clipped, Tuscany voice was like a machine gun firing short bursts of words in my ear. 'Got a bit of a thrash on tomorrow night. Public relations exercise. Feed 'em, wine 'em, flatter 'em. You know the form.'

'Sir.'

'Turn of the Jewish community this time round. Always a bit tricky. Could use your support if you'd care to come.'

I smiled to myself, visualizing that chiselled face with bushy eyebrows and a granite chin. The Jewish community was small but influential. Perhaps because they held the purse strings of the island's economy. In Cyprus – and everywhere else for that matter – when money talks prudent men listen. Or pretend to. 'That's very civil of you, sir,' I said.

'You'll come, then?'

'My pleasure.'

'Um. Maybe. Matter of fact I've got a chap coming I'd like your opinion on.'

I grimaced. Business with pleasure. The doctor's bête noire.

'Odd sort of bird,' Paulus said. 'Bar-Jeshua or Joshua or some such outlandish name. Prefers to use the Greek form. Elymas. Religious as all get out and clever with it.'

'A trouble-maker?'

'Not sure. A disturbing influence though. Got the rabbis in his pocket. Knows it, too.'

'Sounds interesting,' I said politely.

'Up your street, anyway. Seven-thirty for eight. Mess kit, if you please. Got to show the flag, eh?' He rang off before I could reply.

We met in the Residency; an old Turkish fort modernized in the Roman style. Lots of marble staircases, fountains,

Greek repro statuary, mosaic-patterned floors. And in the dining-room, a table as long as the flight deck on a carrier.

Most of Paulus's staff officers were there, their uniforms bright splashes of colour among the dinner jackets and black ties of the civilians – Jewish to a man, skull caps on their heads, diamond rings on their fingers, gold in their teeth. The rabbis were in ceremonial robes, of course, clustering round a thin-faced man with dangerous eyes and an even more dangerous smile.

'That's the feller,' Paulus said as we went in to dine. 'Elymas.'

'Looks very full of himself,' I said diplomatically.

'Full of tricks, too,' Paulus growled.

About sixty of us sat down to eat. All men. Paulus was of the old school: no women in the mess. I was on his left at the head of the table, a corpulent Jewish banker on his right in the place of honour. As I said, Paulus was a stickler for protocol.

The white-tunicked mess stewards were serving the main course when I spotted Troax. He was about halfway down the table, just above the salt, with a rabbi on one side of him and an unremarkable man who looked like a grocer on the other. I wondered how he had managed to get himself invited and decided he had probably gate-crashed with his usual disregard for formalities. He was picking disinterestedly at his food, talking non-stop. The buzz of conversation was loud. Sixty people with good food in front of them and good wine inside them make a lot of noise and I could not hear what he was saying. But I saw the eagerness in his face, the quick movements of his hands and knew he was in full cry on his favourite – indeed his only – subject: Jesus Davidson. I glanced at Paulus and was relieved to see him in earnest conversation with the banker. As well he could not hear Troax. He was not one to tolerate religious talk at his table. No shop in the mess. No politics. No religion. That was the army way.

As our plates were removed and the dessert served there was a lull in the talking. A moment or two of silence which some of my colleagues insist only happens at twenty minutes to the hour. It was broken by a taunting, drawling voice, half-amused, half-bored.

'Personally, Mr Troax,' Elymas said, facing him across the table, 'I find your ideas infantile. Miracles I can stomach, although with some reservations. Healing by faith – yes, perhaps. But a resurrection from the dead?' He shook his head slowly, insultingly. 'If that's the foundation of your heresy I can only express embarrassed astonishment that a man of your obvious education should give it credence. I mean, my dear fellow, dead men don't rise. Even ignorant superstitious women know that.'

All down the table heads were turning to look at Troax. He sat upright, his face pale with anger. Out of the corner of my eye I saw Paulus stiffen, his chin jutting ominously, his mouth a thin, hard line. I waited for the inevitable explosion. But when it came, it came not from the governor but from Troax. Eyes blazing, he sprang to his feet, the heavy wooden chair toppling with a crash behind him. 'You fool.' His voice was sharp as a spear and as wounding. 'Who are you to patronize me?'

It was the opening thrust in a sustained verbal attack which had Elymas squirming in his scat. An attack all the more impressive for being delivered with icy control. Listening to him we forgot his lack of stature, his ugliness of his face, his ill-fitting suit; saw only a brilliant orator dominating us with effortless ease, pricking our consciences, rowelling our self-esteem, shaming our smug élitism. With a skill a high-court barrister would have envied he exposed Elymas' drawling insolence for the empty sham it was, ridiculed his intellectual vanity and demolished him. A tour de force which climaxed in a ringing denunciation: 'You are a man of darkness and deceit. A false prophet who, having ears cannot hear, having eyes cannot see. A blind man leading the blind. And for you, Elymas, the black pit yawns.'

Elymas sat stricken, white-faced and shaking; a broken man stripped of his authority. As Troax finished speaking and stood, hands on hips, staring at him, Elymas raised his head, his face working. He blinked, rubbed his eyes and blinked again. Then he stumbled to his feet with a hoarse cry. 'My eyes. Dear, merciful God, I'm blind. I'm blind.'

He turned and would have fallen had not two of the stewards caught him and led him from the room. The man sitting next to Troax made to follow him but Troax put a hand on his arm. 'No, Barnabas. Not yet. Leave him for now.'

Beside me, Paulus took a deep breath, his face suffused with anger. Troax looked up the table towards him. 'I'm sorry to have spoiled your party, sir,' he said calmly, politely. 'But it had to be done. His mind is warped by a dark and evil spirit, every thought tainted with pride, every idea twisted.'

'Is he really blind?' Paulus said harshly.

'Oh, yes. Totally blind. But tomorrow my friend here will visit him. God will let his light shine on him and restore his sight – and his soul.'

One of the rabbis said indignantly, 'I must protest most

strongly. This has been a disgraceful exhibition by a man of no standing or...'

Troax cut him short. 'You're a brave man, Rabbi, to question the power of the God you serve.'

The rabbi opened his mouth – and closed it again. He had no answer to that.

Paulus stood up, taking command. He beckoned to Troax. 'A word with you, sir.' And it was all there in his voice and bearing; authority, discipline, the hint of a threat. He nodded to me. 'You too, Lucas.'

The three of us went into his study, leaving the ruined dinner party, the nervous, scandalized guests. We stood in the book-lined room and were not invited to sit down.

'I don't believe I know your name, sir,' Paulus said coldly.

'I am Paul Troax.' Troax gave him a little bow. 'An emissary of my Master in whose name I am here tonight.'

'And he is?'

'Jesus. The Jewish Messiah, the Greek Christ.'

Paulus frowned. 'You are here as an interloper without invitation. As such you have insulted my guests, caused one of them serious physical harm and done a great deal of damage to the good relations we have in this island with the Jewish community. And for that I can have you flogged and deported.'

Troax met his eyes levelly. 'I think not, sir. I am a free-born Roman citizen.'

'What?'

I said quietly, 'I know this man, sir. What he says is true.'

'A Roman and a Jew?' Paulus said trying to come to terms with it.

'A Jewish Christian and a Roman, yes.'

'I see,' Paulus said but plainly didn't. 'And this — this Christ of yours — he can take a man's sight from him?'

'And restore it as easily.' Troax spread his hands. 'A small miracle for one who can defeat death itself.'

Paulus's mouth tightened. 'Don't play games with me, man. Defeat death indeed. No man can do that.'

'I didn't believe it either,' Troax said calmly, 'until he opened my eyes to the truth of it.'

Paulus shook his head, puzzled; a bear troubled by a wasp. 'What's that supposed to mean? And before you answer I advise you to be careful.'

I said, 'Mr Troax was also blind. And subsequently regained his sight. I know this to be true. I was there when it happened.'

'I have your word on that, Lucas? As a Roman officer?'

'And as a doctor who could do nothing to help him.'

Paulus rubbed his chin, out of his depth. 'Not a trick?'

'Not a trick.' I remembered the despair in that ugly face, the weeping, sightless eyes.

'Hmm,' Paulus said. 'Well, this puts a different complexion on things. I think we should sit down and talk about it, gentlemen. Rationally. Dispassionately. As intelligent men.'

Troax grinned happily. 'With the greatest of pleasure, sir.'

Troax leaned against the wall behind his bed. 'What a night that was, Michael. My first big breakthrough.'

I smiled. We had talked until dawn. Or rather, Troax had. Taking us through the career of Jesus Davidson from the carpenter's bench in Nazareth, through three years of miracle and hope and wild popularity. All the inspired speeches, all the distilled wisdom, all the astonishing new ideas — to that mockery of a trial at midnight before the Sanhedrin and the cruel death on the eve of the Passover and the rising in splendour on Easter Day. Telling it with skill and a kind of unworldly logic ('He had to die, as we must die, and rise again as, by his grace, we too shall rise') which at one level was totally improbable and at another, deeper, level triumphantly fulfilling. All the questions answered, all the doubts swept away.

'Nothing like starting at the top,' I said. 'A Roman general and a governor to boot.'

'And not a Jew.' Troax's face lit up with the old fervour. 'That's the point. From agnostic to believer in one great leap of faith. Not that Sergius Paulus made a song and dance about it. He remained a covert Christian until his death. But an honest one and practical, sharing his faith with trusted friends. Took the pressure off the Cypriot believers. Gave them the freedom to worship, the same privileges he afforded the Jews on the island.' He sighed. 'Yes, that was a good night's work.'

But it hadn't always been so easy.

4

I flew out of Cyprus the day after that disrupted dinner party in the Residency, heading east to the Remus Airborne Division depot.

Sitting in the rather basic cabin of the old Hermes (Transport Command's workhorse) I reviewed the events of the previous evening and Troax's lucid account of the career of Jesus Davidson. Much of the excitement he had generated in me had faded, but one astonishing fact remained: his absolute conviction, against all logic, all medical experience, that Davidson had risen from his tomb, appeared to his friends, commissioned them to spread the news of his resurrection and subsequently returned to them in spirit to enable them to do this. It was all totally unbelievable – a religious myth to end all myths – until I remembered the transformation of the little, irascible Jew from Tarsus into a towering personality bursting with energy, possessed of an enormous fiery power. I had no explanation for this, but it haunted me and would not go away.

Fabian, the senior MO at Remus, was waiting for me when we landed. I had come in response to an urgent signal from him to act as an expert witness at the court martial of a young paratrooper charged with cowardice. On the face of it, a straightforward case. The man had twelve combat jumps behind him. Tough and fit and in line for promotion. But the week before he had refused to jump.

'Not from fear,' Fabian said. 'I'm convinced of that. He

wanted to jump but couldn't. It's some kind of mental block.'

'You've said as much to the Colonel?'

'Of course. But he doesn't want to know. He sees it as a personal betrayal of trust. An insult to him and to the troops. He's determined to make an example of the boy to restore morale.'

'Ah,' I said. 'One of those.'

'He's a good commander, Mike, and a brilliant soldier. But he has no imagination. No understanding of what makes a man tick. That's why I asked for you. We need an expert to convince the court.'

'You want the charge dropped?'

'Pending a full psychological report, yes. Maybe you can knock some sense into the colonel's head. I can't.'

I nodded doubtfully. Para colonels tend to be suspicious of shrinks and the jargon we talk.

'If they find against him...' Fabian shrugged; a distinguished physician, broad-minded, sympathetic. Qualities which would have put him in the major league in civvy street but were crassly underrated in the army.

'Not a lot of room for manoeuvre, then.' Cowardice in the face of the enemy was a capital offence. Even if the enemy was only a bunch of ragged desert tribesmen preying on military convoys between the Caspian and the Gulf. 'How long have we got, Guy?'

'The court convenes at 10.00 hours the day after tomorrow.'

'What's the man's name?'

'Maxton.'

'Have you tried talking to him?'

'We all have. His company commander, his troop sergeant, me.'

'And?'

'Nothing. He's locked away inside himself. Out of touch. Out of reach.'

My heart sank. When a man cuts himself off from the world, retreats into his own mind and refuses to talk, you need time and patience to win his confidence, establish a rapport with him. Days, not hours. 'We'd best get started then. Where is he? In sick quarters?'

'In the cells. Colonel's orders.'

But when the sergeant of the guard unlocked the steel door for us it was already too late. Maxton had torn his shirt into strips, knotted them together and hanged himself from the bars across the high window.

'Sorry you've had a wasted journey, Lucas,' the Colonel said in the mess that evening. But he looked more relieved than sorry. 'Nasty business. Bad for morale. One rotten apple and all that, eh?'

Justification by clichés, I thought, and wondered if he would write to the next of kin. And what he would say. 'I understand he was a good soldier, sir,' I said tightly, hating his cropped bullet head, the ribbons on his tunic, the bleakness of his eyes.

His lip curled. 'Good soldiers don't funk jumping with their mates when the green light flashes. Only a coward does that. And takes the coward's way out.'

I looked him in the eye. 'His company commander tells me he was very promising.'

'So he appeared, but...'

'Promising enough to have been hospitalized for observation and therapy. Not thrown into a cell. Your orders, I believe?'

He nodded. 'Pending trial as laid down in ER's.'

'Of course. Everything by the book. Mentally disturbed. Locked in solitary confinement. No medical tests. No definite diagnosis. Nothing proved. I shall emphasize that in my report.'

He stiffened. 'I think that would be very unwise, Lucas.'

'Just doing my job, sir. Hoping for co-operation from commanders concerned about the welfare of their men. That's why I was brought in. Too late.'

'I've already apologized to you for that. And reprimanded the sergeant of the guard for slackness.'

'Bolted the stable door after the horse has gone. Yes, I'm sure.'

His face reddened. 'Look, I don't have to listen to this. The man's dead and that's the end of it.'

'I wouldn't bank on that, sir. I think you'll find these things look very different in GHQ.' I had the small satisfaction of seeing his eyes flicker uneasily.

It was all bluff, of course, and he knew it. But I had touched a nerve. Perhaps the next man who refused to jump would receive better treatment.

He turned his back on me and stamped away. I collected a large whisky from the bar and stood looking round the ante-room, now full of officers. They carefully pretended not to see me, unwilling to fraternize with a stranger who had obviously fallen foul of their CO. I didn't blame them. They had to live with him. I decided it would be politic (and more enjoyable) to eat out, finished my drink and made for the door. As I was picking up my cap from the lobby table, a voice behind me said, 'You're Lucas, aren't you?'

I turned to face him. An inch or so shorter than I, he

was yet an impressive figure, broad-shouldered, solidly built, wearing his uniform with a certain rakish élan. I saw the insignia of a full brigadier on his shoulders, the proud badges of the 1st Armoured Division on his lapels, the impressive row of ribbons on his chest.

'We're out of place among these Para thugs,' he said. 'Yes?'

I nodded, liking the deep voice, the bright eyes, the warmth of him.

'There's a half-decent restaurant in the town. Well, a decent restaurant with half-decent waitresses. My car's outside if you'd care to join me for dinner? I'm Brigadier Ferris, by the way.'

We sat in the rear seat behind his sergeant driver, the sentries on the gate presenting arms as we drove through.

'I was at the bar when you were putting Colonel Constans in his place,' he said. 'Couldn't help overhearing.' He chuckled. 'I imagine it's been a long time since anyone below my rank stood up to him the way you did.' He raised his hand. 'No, don't apologize. You were quite right. The man's a bully. Good at his job, impossible to live with.'

'Or die for,' I said, still simmering a little.

'The young para?' He nodded. 'A difficult case badly handled. I've been doing my homework on you, Lucas. A much-travelled man, I find.'

'Goes with the job, sir.'

'At which, I'm told, you're an expert. D'you enjoy it?'

I said I did, wondering where all this was leading. An off-the-record discussion of some ailment, perhaps?

'Ever thought of changing to something more – well, challenging?'

I shook my head. 'I'm doing what I've always wanted to do. What I'm best at.'

'Could you have helped him?'

'The para? I don't know. A mind stretched beyond its limits is not easily healed. I'd've needed time – quite a lot of time.'

'But his time ran out before you even saw him.' Ferris shook his head. 'Stupid waste.'

Outside the restaurant he told his driver not to wait. 'Busy day tomorrow, Sar'nt. We'll take a cab back to the base.' It was something Constans would never have said.

As we went inside, he had a quiet word with the maître d', who found us a table in a small alcove. The food, when it came, was very good. He was right about the waitresses too.

'I brought Constans here once,' Ferris said. 'Never again. He ate like a pig and pinched the girls' bottoms.'

Conduct unbecoming, I thought, concealing a grin.

He was an excellent host with a fund of good stories and shrewd comments which carried us comfortably through to the coffee and liqueurs. I understood the softening technique designed to relax me and was not altogether surprised when he said, out of the blue, 'Does the name Troax mean anything to you? Paul Troax?' His voice was still casual but his eyes were suddenly sharp.

Wondering if he had been in touch with Paulus, I said carefully, 'With respect, sir, before I answer that, why do you ask?'

He gave me a quick, approving grin. 'A prudent question. Deserves an honest answer. Can I rely on your professional discretion as a doctor if I give you one?'

'I know how to keep a confidence.'

He nodded. 'I'm sure. Well then, I'm interested in

Troax because he intrigues me.' He saw my surprise. 'I
know. Why should an old tank man be intrigued by a
Jewish civilian, eh?'

'Something like that, yes.'

He glanced down at his tunic. 'I don't drive a tank
these days, Lucas. I drive a desk in GHQ. CI2, to be
precise.'

'Ah,' I said. He didn't look like a spy master. But then,
they never do.

'Well?'

'Yes, I know Troax.' I gave him a brief summary of
what I knew, from that day in Damascus to the dinner
party for the Jews of Cyprus.

'So what's your opinion of the feller?'

I said, cautiously, 'He's possessed of a dream. A
religious dream of freedom and peace, first promulgated
by a Nazarene carpenter in defiance of orthodox Jewry.'

'Davidson, you mean?' Ferris shrugged dismissively.
'Pilate had him topped to keep the Sanhedrin happy.
File closed.'

'Not quite. You know he was seen alive by his friends
three days later?'

Ferris's mouth tightened. 'I know the grave was robbed
by his followers and the rumour of his resurrection
spread around. Nonsense, of course. Dead men don't
come back, Lucas. You, of all people, should know that.
They've probably got the corpse mummified and placed
in a hidden shrine somewhere in the Galilean hills. That
I can understand. But alive again?' He shook his head.
'Nobody in his right mind'd believe that.'

'Troax does.'

'He's one of them, is he?'

'With all the zeal of a convert. He's got ambitions to

turn an obscure Jewish sect into a world religion open to all races.'

'You're quite sure of that?'

'Why else would he turn up in Cyprus? The first stepping-stone to Turkey. And beyond.'

Ferris nodded slowly. 'That's what I've heard. Why I'm interested.' He thought for a moment, frowning. 'A religious splinter group in a backwater of the Empire is of little interest to my department. We deal in facts, not fantasies in which dead men come back to life. But a political movement, disguised as religion, intent to undermine the authority of the Pax Romana – we're very interested in that.'

I shook my head. 'It's only political in the sense that it's loyal to a leader who proclaimed a new kingdom greater than Rome. That's what he taught. A kingdom not of this world.'

'But in it?'

'Oh yes. Very much so. With its own culture, its own credo.'

'And its own king?'

I nodded. 'Jesus, the King not just of the Jews, as Pilate thought, but of the world.'

'Do you, by any chance, share that belief?'

'No. But that's not the point, is it? The Christians believe it. And none more fervently than Troax. Remember, Davidson had been dead almost two years when, according to Troax, he restored his sight.'

'How? You're the doctor, Lucas. You must have a theory about it.'

'I wish I had. All this sort of rumoured power needs to kill it stone dead is a rational, psychological explanation. So far as I know there isn't one.'

'Yes, I see.' Ferris signalled for more coffee. When the girl brought it, he said, 'So what we have here is a secret society of people whose leader, religious or political, is a ghost.'

'A spirit, yes.'

'There's a difference?'

I nodded. 'A ghost is a shadow, a memory. And memories fade quickly in the face of opposition. Few men will die for a ghost. But a spirit is inside a man. In his head, in his heart, in what the religious call his soul. And a spirit thrives on opposition, adversity, persecution. The harder we try to stamp it out, the stronger it becomes. We can control people's actions. But we can't control their thoughts and beliefs. If we put them to death, the spirit lives on in their children. We can destroy them, but we can't destroy the spirit. If there is, as you suppose, a secret society, that is its secret.'

'Hmm.' Ferris frowned. 'That's what I feared. With good reason, apparently.' He sipped his coffee. 'And what you're saying is, Troax is possessed by this militant spirit?'

I smiled. 'I don't think the spirit is militant. Davidson certainly wasn't. There was an army of Jewish terrorists – the Freedom Fighters – poised to move on his command. But astonishingly he rejected them and went to his death without resistance. A man of peace and forgiveness.'

Ferris looked at me blankly, unable to visualize such a man.

'Troax, on the other hand, is very militant, fighting for his faith with what appear to be supernatural powers.'

'Yes. All my information points to that. Which is why I'm talking to you now, Lucas. If, as seems likely, Troax's venture into Cyprus is only the opening shot in a campaign reaching out across the Mediterranean into the heart of the Empire, then we have a problem on our hands. And a very ugly one. Cyprus today, Turkey tomorrow, Greece next week, Rome itself when?'

I said, 'One man, sir. A remarkable man with a silver tongue and totally without fear. But still, just one man.' I shook my head. 'Not enough to destroy the army.'

'And if the words turn to bombs?' Ferris said sombrely.

'That's not his line, sir. I'm sure of that.'

'Maybe. But there are other ways. Supposing he moves across the provinces, creating cells in every town and city he visits, establishing a foothold in the community, spreading dissension by acts of civic disobedience? On the surface he's just a wandering preacher with a particularly unlikely credo. But underneath he could be an agent provocateur, filling the heads of the common people – the poor, the underprivileged – with wild ideas of conquest. Laying the foundations of a subversive movement which could topple Rome.' Ferris shook his head.

'It's not on, Lucas. If Troax were just a renegade Jew we could close him down tomorrow. But he's also one of us. A Roman citizen entitled to freedom of speech, to go wherever he chooses in the Empire. Puts us in an awkward position if we want to neutralize him.'

'I understand what you're saying, sir, but...'

He cut me short. 'Good. Because I want you to help us. You're in a unique position to do so. An MO conducting a major research programme into the psychological problems of our troops. Like Troax, you're a free agent travelling the world from base to base, hospital to hospital.' He leaned forward across the table.

'What I want you to do is keep track of Troax on his trail-blazing expeditions, reporting directly to me on everything he says and does. The kind of reception he gets. The people he recruits. The cells he establishes and nurses. It won't interfere with your official duties and it will keep me up-to-date on the strength of these – what d'you call 'em?'

'Christians.'

'Right. He's bound to come unstuck eventually. People with an ego as outsize as his always do. I want to know when it happens and where. Ideally in advance.' He sat back, folding his arms. 'Well, what d'you say?'

I hesitated, not relishing the role of informer but aware of the logic of his proposition and of the threat to Rome of an underground movement loyal to Davidson and his alternative kingdom. 'It's not something I've ever contemplated doing, sir. I'm neither a religious nor a political animal.'

'Just a damned good expert in your own field with no personal axe to grind. Tuned into the minds of our lads at the sharp end – our first line of defence against those barbarians in Europe. And a loyal citizen of Rome.'

I smiled. 'You flatter me, sir.'

'No, Lucas. I tell it the way it is. If you decide to join the Firm you'll quickly realize that flattery is not a weapon I use. Will you? Join us, I mean?'

'You want my answer now?'

He nodded. 'If you can't make up your mind tonight you're no use to me.'

'All right. I'll take it on, sir.'

He grinned, openly pleased. 'Good man. I'm leaving for Athens at first light. I'll be back in my office in Rome in a couple of days. My secretary will send you the necessary documentation – identification papers, fax numbers, code books – and write you on to the Firm. Stay on here until the package comes through. Fabian'll find you something to do while you're waiting, I'll make sure of that before I go. Constans won't like you hanging around but he'll have to lump it. And by the way, you'd better visit the base tailor tomorrow.'

'Sir?' I said, puzzled.

'As of 09.00 hours you'll be Colonel Lucas. Give you a bit more clout with the civic bigwigs out in the sticks.'

'I'll be operating in uniform then?'

'Of course. Nobody's going to expect a doctor to be one of my boys.' He put out his hand. 'Welcome to the Firm, Mike.'

'Thank you very much, sir.'

He met my eyes steadily. 'I'm not a hard man, you'll find. Just a demanding one.'

And so it was to prove.

The coded fax came into Remus within twenty-four hours of the arrival of the information pack from Ferris's secretary. I used the code book to decipher it.

As you are in the area you might do a recce in
Lystra. Troax is due there sometime today. I want
to know why. F.

It quite spoiled Constans' breakfast. I caught him glaring at me down the table, obviously trying to fathom why a medic should receive coded signals from GHQ. And beginning to worry seriously about the report he thought I had written. I fended off his clumsy questions politely, murmuring vaguely about my Hippocratic oath.

'Oh, I see. It's medical, is it,' he said harshly, '*Colonel* Lucas?'

'What else?' I said, and let him stew.

Fabian ran me into Antioch. The controller at the fighter base there accepted my story of an urgent case in Lystra and laid on a chopper from the rescue flight. I found myself wishing Troax had been with me at Remus to set the young para free from his trauma. And grinned to myself, imagining Constans' reaction to that fiery little Jew bristling with astonishing power.

Lystra is a typical Greco-Roman town with little to commend it. One or two impressive buildings in the centre, a reasonably prosperous business community and the usual squalid slums. I booked in for a couple of nights at the leading hotel, ate a passable lunch and went out to find Troax. Not a difficult task. Wherever there was a crowd he would be in the middle of it. A one-role actor hungry for an audience.

The main square was dominated by a huge, mock-Doric temple to Zeus (Lystra is in the old-time religion belt) brooding over the market stalls. That was where the people were. And there was Troax with big, earnest Barnabas, working his way through the crowd, looking for an excuse to go into his spiel. He found it in the unlikely person of Dimos.

Dimos was a professional beggar; a pathetic bundle of rags and sores squatting at the foot of the temple steps on a battered wooden trolley fitted with pram wheels, his tin mug in his hand, his hair lank and greasy with dirt, his face crawling with flies. Not a pleasant sight. Even the people who dropped coins into his mug looked the other way as they did so. Held their breath, too, probably. The man was filthy. But Troax made straight for him, striding down between the stalls in that purposeful, jaunty walk of his with Barnabas in tow like a minder. He stopped in front of Dimos and looked him full in the face.

The beggar rattled his tin hopefully and went into his whining routine for alms. But Troax cut him short. 'This won't do,' he said sharply. 'This is no way to live, my friend. You've got legs, man. Use them. In the name of God's Son, get up and walk.'

Dimos gaped at him. A voice in the crowd shouted derisively, 'You might as well tell a pig to fly, mate. He's never walked in his life.'

'Come on, man. Up.' Troax's voice cut through the titters like the crack of a whip. I saw the tension in his face, his eyes blazing.

And suddenly, incredibly, Dimos was on his feet, swaying a little but upright. His legs, thin and wasted by years of inactivity, visibly straightened. The slack muscles filled out, flexing and bunching under the dirty skin. His bare toes gripped the cobbles and he was balanced, poised.

'That's better.' Troax kicked the trolley away. 'Now walk.'

And Dimos walked. A tentative shuffle at first as he found his balance. And then he was off. He took the temple steps two at a time, turned at the top to face the crowd, raised clasped hands above his head in triumph and came leaping down again. Sure-footed, nimble, laughing with excitement.

The crowd received him rapturously, dancing and singing in a great circle round him while he pirouetted, arms outstretched, head thrown back, lank hair flying. The women raided the flower stalls to make garlands for

Troax and Barnabas. Men ran to the cattle pens and dragged out an ox to sacrifice to Zeus.

As if on cue, the priest appeared in the temple doorway; a deus ex machina in white robes and a scarlet stole. The people greeted him with shouts of praise, touching foreheads and chests in reverent salute. Standing half-hidden in the shadow of a pillar, I could see his face clearly and watch his eyes. Dark hooded eyes, shrewd, calculating. The eyes of an opportunist. It was a moment of high drama and he knew it. One ill-considered word and he would lose his authority, upstaged by two Jewish strangers who had worked some kind of a miracle on his doorstep. A miracle he could not emulate.

He raised his arms in blessing, assumed an expression of pious wonder and walked slowly down the steps. The people fell silent, opening to let him through, and he bowed to Troax and Barnabas, kissed their hands and led them up the steps. Standing beside them, facing the crowd, he said in an awed voice, 'The gods have come among us this day. Great Zeus himself in human guise.' He nodded respectfully to Barnabas. 'And his eloquent spokesman, Hermes.' He nodded to Troax.

There was a tiny, breathless pause, broken only by the mournful lowing of the ox scenting death. Everything hung now on the people's reaction.

'We are in the presence of the Immortals,' the priest said.

Then the crowd gave a great shout and fell to their knees in homage and fear.

I saw Troax's eyes flash in anger. His head came up, his fists clenched hard at his sides. Now, I thought. Now's your chance to turn a religious mystery into a political triumph. The priest has transferred his authority to you. All you have to do is exploit it and the town is yours for the taking.

And I thought: Is this how it all begins? The first blow against Rome struck here out in the open in a small, Turkish town full of poor, oppressed people with nothing to lose and everything to gain?

'No!' Troax's voice rang out like a tocsin over the kneeling figures below him. 'People of Lystra, why are you doing this? We are mortal men as you are. Messengers not of Zeus but of the one true God, Creator of heaven and earth. He alone is to be worshipped. He who sent his Son, Jesus, to live and die among us and rise again to open the gates of the Kingdom, that all who believe in him might enter and find eternal life.'

I watched the people standing up, heard their murmuring, sensed their disappointment. You've blown it, I thought. Told them too much too soon. You had them in the palm of your hand and you've let them slip through your fingers.

The priest said suavely, 'Modestly said, sir. But you healed Dimos the cripple. See how he stands and walks among us. Only Zeus could do that.'

Troax fell headlong into the trap, his quick temper flaring. 'Zeus is a myth, invented by men like you to batten on the poor and weak whilst making yourself rich and powerful. The God whom we serve is the only God, the ultimate reality. He is not interested in your blood sacrifices. He takes no pleasure in your rites and ceremonies. He asks only that we should trust and honour him and live in peace together, sharing what we have in his name.'

The people hesitated, murmuring together, uncertain. The priest smiled thinly, hatred in his eyes. He had been discredited in front of the town, his rituals scorned, his god treated with contempt. But it was still his town and he knew how to handle it. 'I am the priest of Zeus.' He drew himself up, dwarfing Troax. 'He is our god and we will have no other. I received you with honour and you have tricked me. Tricked us all with your evil magic. You come here masquerading as gods and I have exposed you for the charlatans you are. We don't need your kind in Lystra, Jew. Not you nor your Jewish god.' He turned to the crowd. 'Away with them. They are cheats and liars. Blasphemers. Trouble-makers. Away with them, I say.'

The people erupted with a great roar of anger, prised up cobblestones with their knives, dragged Troax and Barnabas down and began to pelt them. In seconds they were overwhelmed, huddled together on the ground, cut and bruised and bleeding. The crowd swarmed over them, kicking, stamping, spitting on them. The priest watched impassively as they were dragged across the square to the town gate, thrown bodily out on to the road and left for dead.

'Now bring me the ox,' the priest shouted, 'and let its blood cleanse the town of this evil...'

The small, frail figure on the bed smiled now; the same defiant, slightly rueful smile he had given me through half-closed eyes and swollen lips that long-ago night in Lystra. 'I expect you'd have handled it differently, Michael.'

I grinned. 'On-the-spot cures are not my line. I'd've had to spend a lot of time on Dimos. Give him a course of therapy. Always assuming his problem was mental, not physical. Was it?'

Troax shrugged. 'That's not a question I ask. I heal the soul. God heals the body.' He shook his head. 'These things come by prayer and fasting. A gift of God.' He tilted his head. 'As you well know, old friend.'

I nodded. The little Jewish–Christian community in Lystra had waited until the sacrifice of the ox was in full swing, the priest pulling out all his ritualistic stops. And then slipped out to collect the two of them and smuggle them into the ghetto. I had followed them and offered my services as a doctor, cleansing their wounds, bandaging them, prescribing hot soup and rest, promising to look in again the next morning. But when I went back they had already gone.

My coded fax to Ferris had been tersely reassuring, describing the incident as a religious act with no political undertones. The consequences unpleasant but quickly contained by the priest. And he had accepted that.

'You were in no state to travel, though,' I said.

He shrugged. 'They were in danger. Harbouring malcontents. It wouldn't have been fair to them for us to stay. I mean, we were just passing through but they had to live there, their children hostages to fortune, their jobs on the line.' He tapped his writing pad. 'I'm still in touch with them, y'know. Listening to their problems, trying to nourish their churchmanship. They and all the others like them, bravely bearing their witness in so many towns, so many provinces. I think of them as my family.' He put his hand on mine for a moment. 'And of you as my brother.'

'I know,' I said, unable to meet his eyes. I knew I was

going to have to tell him why I had come. But not yet.
I wasn't ready yet. Would I ever be?

5

Just before three the guard on the landing came in without knocking and dumped a basket on the bed.

'What's this?' I said sharply.

'Biscuits and a thermos of coffee.' He grinned, thick-lipped, crop-headed, his eyes small and pale. The sort of redcap who gave the military police a bad name. 'From his girlfriends. All checked out. No weapons. No drugs.'

'Sir,' I said warningly.

He looked at me sullenly. 'Sir.' And turned to leave.

'The next time you come in, knock first and wait.'

He stiffened, anger in his eyes. 'Sir.'

'Out,' I said.

He stamped out, locking the door on us.

'Ill-mannered brute,' I said.

Troax shrugged. 'Just doing his job, Michael.'

We shared the coffee but I left the biscuits to Troax. He ate them hungrily, tasted his coffee and said, 'You're here for my trial, I take it?'

I hesitated. Had he heard something of what Nero was planning for him. 'Trial?' I said warily.

'That's why you brought me here four years ago. Remember?'

From the cell in Caesarea where he had been held in chains for two years until Agrippa had come to the throne of Israel. Two years without freedom of movement, with no audience to inspire him. 'Only because you insisted on your rights as a Roman, Paul.'

One of the better puppet kings, tolerant, liberal, with a real concern for his subjects, Agrippa had wanted to set him free, impressed by his integrity, moved by his single-minded zeal. But Troax had stubbornly refused his pardon, demanding to be tried before the Emperor himself. A trial he could use as a platform to say his piece in the heart of the Empire. He had been transported to Italy with an armed escort and I had sailed with him. Ferris had made sure of that, determined to milk him dry of information before the lawyers got at him.

'I know,' he said now. 'I'm not blaming you, Michael. But four years in this stinking chicken coop waiting for justice — it's been a long time.'

'Too long,' I said. But it was not the miserable attic which irked him, the meagre rations, the lack of company. It was the irony of being where he had always wanted to be — the greatest city in the world — yet powerless to exploit his position, put Christianity on the map. I shrugged. 'You know what Nero's like. Paranoiac. Every day a new enemy, a new threat to his authority. You're a long way down his list by now. The chances are he's forgotten all about you.'

He didn't like that, his pride affronted. 'Is that what you're here to tell me? That I'm a spent force? An insignificant nobody not worth the expense of a trial? Because if it is you're wasting your time. I won't accept it. I'm a Roman citizen and I want my day in court, the charges dismissed, a public apology given. The rights of Christians recognized and honoured. Not just my personal freedom. The freedom of all my people.'

'I know,' I said, a Judas come to betray him. 'The way it was in Philippi, eh?'

'Busy little bee, ain't he?' Ferris growled.

It was the summer of 51 and we were standing in his

office in the Via Flavia studying the wall map of the Eastern Mediterranean; a map dotted with blue circles tracing Troax's progress. Salamis, Perga, Antioch, Lystra, Derbe. In all these towns he had established Christian cells; his churches, as he called them. Small groups of believers drawn mainly from the working class, meeting behind closed doors in each other's houses to sing and pray and celebrate their secret love-feast. Individually of little account. But linked together in a chain forged by Troax...

'He gets around,' I said.

'And now he's heading west to Troas, you say?' A little port on the north-east coast of the Aegean. 'I don't like the look of that. It's a short hop from there to the Balkans and Greece.'

'I doubt he'll do that, sir. Turkey's his home ground. My hunch is he'll consolidate his hold there.' But I didn't believe it. Nor did Ferris. Troax was a pioneer, not a consolidator. A restless spirit unable to resist the lure of new horizons.

'Um. Maybe. Has he still got that other feller with him?'

'Barnabas? No. They fell out a while back. Clash of personalities. Barnabas walked out and went back to Cyprus. He's the cautious type. Plenty of bottle but no imagination. I think Troax scares him a bit.'

'He doesn't do much for my peace of mind either,' Ferris said. 'He's trouble, Lucas. Your reports prove that. Wherever he goes he makes waves. Upsets the civic fathers. Infuriates the Jewish ghetto leaders.'

'They think he's a heretic.'

'And I think he's a political agitator.'

It was a point of view I could not altogether dismiss.

All Troax's speeches fell into that category. Words of peace edged like swords. Down with the rich and powerful. God is on the side of the poor, the hungry, the despised. There's a choice between two masters – God and Caesar. Nobody can serve them both. Caesar's in Rome, remote, uncaring. God is in your hearts and minds, sharing your anxieties, your misery. Waiting to set you free to live with dignity and hope.

However skilfully those ideas were presented as religious beliefs they were basically revolutionary. An attack on orthodox Jewry, as Caiaphas had understood, or an attack on Rome, as Pilate had unwillingly recognized. East of Rome there was a fine line between religion and politics. A line which Troax crossed every time he opened his mouth. My instinct was to agree with Ferris. But he had not seen Troax the healer in action. I had.

I said, 'He's got no muscle, of course.' And remembered that had been said about Jesus Davidson.

'We don't know that,' Ferris said. 'No active army, certainly. But there may well be a sleeping one waiting for the call to rise.' As the Jewish terrorist gangs – freedom fighters as they called themselves – had waited for a word from Davidson to fall on Jerusalem at the Passover in 33 and drive the legions into the sea. And been disappointed. 'Before he can activate that he needs a firm base this side of the Adriatic.'

'Here in Rome?' I said, knowing it was true, not wanting to believe it.

'Precisely.' Ferris nodded, his face sombre. 'Look at his record, Lucas.' His finger traced the line across the map. 'He's come a long way since Cyprus.'

'And a hard one,' I said.

Ferris shrugged. 'He's a Jew and used to suffering for it. He's unlikely to add to that suffering for a small religious splinter group. But for political freedom, the chance of real power...' He left the sentence ominously unfinished.

'We've no hard evidence of that, sir.' The file on Troax, lying on the desk, was bulky now. It could be read as a document of treasonable activities. But equally it could just be a record of a religious struggle posing no real threat to the State.

'Then get me some,' Ferris rapped. 'The longer he's at liberty the more dangerous he becomes.'

'Annoying,' I said, 'but hardly dangerous.'

Ferris smiled thinly. 'You're a good doctor, Lucas, but politically naïve. Let me tell you something. Empires don't fall spectacularly in battle. They slowly corrode from within, eaten away by secret societies sowing seeds of unrest and disaffection. A hidden cancer difficult to isolate, virtually impossible to contain. Outwardly Rome is strong. But it could easily become an empty shell needing only one decisive blow to smash it.'

'I hear what you're saying, sir.'

'Good.' Ferris opened the file and riffled through it. 'He's on his own now, you say?'

'No. He has another partner. Two, in fact. A Jew called Silas and a young Greek lad – Timothy.'

'Silas. Timothy.' Ferris spat out the names disgustedly. 'Is that the best you can do?'

'I'm sorry. They use only first names. What they call Christian names.'

'Code names, you mean?'

'Perhaps. Silas is a Barnabas look-alike. Conservative, stolid. Without Troax, a nobody.'

'Aren't they all?' Ferris said. 'And the boy?'

I hesitated. The relationship between Troax and Timothy intrigued me professionally. I had seen them together in Antioch, at ease with one another. A classic attraction of opposites, perhaps. Timothy was young, good-looking, a touch too full of himself but likeable. Troax doted on him as if the boy were his son. But I felt it went deeper than that. A shared faith, a common purpose, yes. But there was something else that linked them together. A memory, perhaps...?

Back in the late 30s a sergeant of the Tenth Legion was brought into our military hospital at Haifa. He was deeply traumatized and showing all the symptoms of a mental breakdown. Hallucinations, nightmares, long periods of brooding silence broken by crying fits and sudden brainstorms in which he became very violent, smashing up his room, terrorizing the staff. His case notes from his regimental CO in Jerusalem attributed his condition to an incident he had witnessed in the city a few weeks earlier. A Greek Jew, Stephen Michaelides, on a pilgrimage to Israel, had fallen under the spell of the Davidson cult and had been unwise enough to say so publicly. Troax had been running his anti-heresy squad then and had arrested Michaelides, brought him before the Sanhedrin and charged him with blasphemy. Invited to speak in his own defence, the prisoner had made a virulent attack on the High Priest, condemning him for the murder of Davidson, urging him passionately to repent and follow the teachings of the resurrected Christ. There was only one answer to that. Michaelides was found guilty, taken outside the city wall and stoned by the rabbis. A brutal sentence, brutally carried out.

And Troax had officiated at his death.

'I was the NCO in charge of the burial party,' the sergeant said when, after much patient probing on my part, he began to talk. 'The Jews just left him to rot in the sun.' He looked at me with haunted eyes. 'Death I understand, sir. A bullet in the head if you're lucky, a bayonet in the guts if you're not. It's you or him, see? Quickly done and quickly finished. But stoning.' He shuddered. 'That's a terrible way to kill a man. Slow, barbaric. He was pulped, y'know. Hardly a bone left unbroken in his body. Ripped and torn, smothered in blood. Hardly recognizable as a human being.' His voice cracked over the horror of it. 'What sort of religion would do that to a man, sir? How could those sadistic priests live with themselves afterwards?'

It was a question I had asked myself more than once as I had come to know Troax. That same disciplined zeal which had masterminded the death of Michaelides was now building churches for the God for whom the Greek had been martyred. The risks he took, the hardships he endured – were these a kind of expiation, welcomed as a masochist welcomes the scourge? When I saw him with Timothy in Antioch I wondered if he saw in that eager, handsome boy the reincarnation of Stephen Michaelides and so found relief from his burden of guilt. Two Greeks, both young and innocent. One battered to death, the other received by Troax into the life of the church. It was a coincidence, of course, a quirk of fate. But he would read into it the evidence of forgiveness. It was the sort of convoluted thinking he was adept at. What I had once heard him describe as the mystery of grace...

'Well?' Ferris said impatiently.

I put my thoughts aside. Ferris was interested in facts, not theories. 'Timothy's intelligent, enthusiastic,' I said. As Stephen had been. 'Sees Troax as his hero.'

'And Greek, you say?'

'Yes.'

Ferris nodded glumly. 'It all adds up, doesn't it? Our ugly little firebrand's going to Greece and needs a Greek to back him up, give him a bit of kudos with those eggheads over there.'

'We don't know that, sir.'

'Oh, come on, Lucas. Get a grip. It's obvious, damn it. They'll be booked on the ferry to Neapolis en route for Philippi and the interior. And when they roll in there I want you on the spot.'

I was on Al Italia's morning flight to Philippi the next day and was given a guest room in the Consulate. A phone call to the Customs office in Neapolis confirmed that Ferris had been right about Troax and Silas. They had passed through the previous evening and boarded the coach for Philippi. But he had been wrong about Timothy who had apparently stayed on in Troas. Why?

I changed into civvies and went out to find the answer.

It was like coming home. Philippi is a pleasant city, the streets wide and clean, the buildings genuine Greek, not the clumsy copies seen in Turkey, the people prosperous and businesslike with none of the shifty laziness of the Eastern provincials. My people, with Greek faces and sharp-vowelled Greek voices. I walked through spacious arcades of expensive shops and across neat little squares where fountains played in the sunlight and the bars and restaurants had white-clothed tables on the pavements.

This was Europe; ordered, civilized, sure of itself. What chance did Troax have in a city like this? The people would be repelled by his ugliness and embarrassed by the raw passion of his religion. They preferred an intellectual approach, logical, exploratory, not so much worshipping God as engaging politely in a dialogue about him.

I guessed he would make for the ghetto first, his dream of bringing his own people into the Faith always uppermost in his mind – perhaps because it was a lost cause. But just before I entered it I found him with Silas jauntily walking through a small market, the beginnings of a crowd gathering round them. The little man was talking animatedly in street Greek, smiling, enjoying himself. This was the gentler side of his nature, easy, compassionate, in its way charming. The women loved it, hanging on to his words, infected by his enthusiasm. He was surprisingly popular with women, as Davidson had been. Perhaps because they were both impervious to their sexual attraction, infused with a love which transcended the physical.

You're learning, I thought, watching him. The fire was there but banked down. Warming, not blistering. Creating a rapport the people welcomed and Ferris would worry about.

But it didn't last.

As I tailed along at the back of the crowd we came to a booth in the corner of the market; a black, canvas tent decorated with the signs of the Zodiac cut out of silver paper. The curtain was pulled aside on the front of the booth and a girl sat inside behind a small table on which was a crystal ball. She was young – not more than sixteen and provocatively dressed in a short-skirted, diaphanous frock which left little to the imagination. There were silver bracelets on her wrists and flowers in her long, black hair. Her face was heavily made up: dark red lipstick, black mascara emphasizing huge round eyes, a silver stud in her nose. A pointed, high-cheekboned face old beyond her years and desperately unhappy. A mask reflecting her inner distress.

Two men stood outside the booth urging passers-by to go in and have their fortunes told. They were gaudily dressed in embroidered shirts and baggy black trousers, bandannas tied over their heads, gold rings in their ears. Romanian gypsies with the dark skin and bold, black eyes of their race. Big men, lean and hard.

'Who knows what tomorrow may bring you, my handsomes?' one of them said in a sing-song, wheedling voice only gypsies can produce. 'She does.' He pointed dramatically at the girl. 'She can warn you of dangers, show you the way to happiness and wealth. Why walk blindly into the future? Let her open your eyes and settle your minds. Forewarned is forearmed, my darlings. One silver coin buys you security.'

Troax stopped abruptly outside the booth, a flush of anger darkening his face, the old fire blazing in his eyes.

Here we go again, I thought.

The girl took one look at him, stood up with a shriek of terror and began to babble in a high, eerie voice, surprisingly loud for so slight a person: 'These men are the servants of the Most High who proclaim to you the way of truth and hope.'

A little shiver ran through the crowd. Not because of what she said but of the way she said it. It was as if someone else was speaking. An alien spirit issuing out of her mouth. I saw the red needle marks on her arms and knew she was heavily drugged. The men in charge of her scowled and told her sharply to be quiet. But she cried out all the louder: 'These men are the servants of the Most High who...'

'That's enough.' Troax silenced her in mid-sentence, his voice icy with anger. He turned to face the crowd. 'She's possessed by an evil spirit, poor girl. And these men exploit her misery for money.' He swung round, pointed a finger at her and said with immense authority, 'I charge you in the name of Jesus the Christ to come out of her.'

The girl shuddered in a paroxysm of agony, eyes staring, face contorted. She swayed drunkenly, stiffened in her chair and collapsed over the table. The crystal ball rolled off and shattered on the cobbles. The crowd stood in appalled silence.

One of the gypsies rounded on Troax. 'You've killed her, damn you.'

'No.' Troax smiled, relaxed now. 'I've given her back her life.'

The girl slumped back in her chair, opened her eyes slowly and focused on Troax. 'Oh, sir,' she said and her voice was natural. The voice of a child at peace with herself.

She stood up, pushed the table aside and came out to kneel at Troax's feet, tears of relief streaking the mascara on her face. He touched her head. 'Go in peace, my daughter, and give God the praise.'

I watched, my mind full of questions, as he lifted her up, smiling. Schizophrenics are notoriously difficult to treat, requiring weeks – even months – of therapy with only a ten per cent chance of success. But he had cured her in a moment, calling on a power beyond my comprehension. The same awesome power he had used in Cyprus and Lystra and many more towns. Was this the gift of a carpenter long dead? I found it difficult to believe; knew Ferris would find it impossible.

The crowd began to drift away with many backward glances at Troax and Silas and the girl standing between them. The gypsies appealed to them to stay. 'Please, my dears, be patient. She's a very gifted girl and it sometimes gets too much for her. But she's recovered now, as you can see. Give her a couple of minutes, eh? The first customer will pay nothing.'

As the people wavered, Troax took charge. 'Don't waste your time or your money, my friends. The girl is healed. In her right mind. She'll have nothing to tell you now.'

The bigger of the two gypsies grabbed his arm and spun him round. 'What's your game then, you little runt? Coming here and ruining our business. If you think you can take over our pitch and install this Jesus of yours, forget it.'

'You'd better believe it, Jew-boy,' the other one said.

Troax wrenched his arm free. 'I believe what I believe. I advise you to look for honest work instead of living off the earnings of a poor, deluded girl.' He nodded to Silas. 'Let's go.'

'Not so fast,' the gypsy said, his voice hard. 'There's a little matter of compensation to be settled.'

'I owe you nothing,' Troax said flatly.

The gypsy's hand slipped inside his shirt and came out holding a knife. 'Let's not argue about this, eh?'

'Let's not.' Silas, moving quickly for so solid a man, gripped the man's wrist and twisted it sharply. The knife clattered to the cobbles. Silas kicked it away, forced the man to his knees and released him. 'No need for unpleasantness, surely?' He looked at Troax and they began to walk away, taking the girl with them.

'You'll sing a different song, my handsome,' the gypsy shouted after them, 'when you're up before the beak.'

Which, an hour later, was where they were, standing in the dock in the City Hall facing the magistrates of Philippi.

In the public gallery, anonymous among those around me, I listened to the gypsies laying charges. Doing it smoothly, deferentially, with just the right amount of injured innocence. 'These men are foreign Jews, Your Worships.' That damning racial title, itself sufficient to condemn them. 'They advocate customs which it's not lawful for us to practise.'

A pack of lies, of course, but utterly convincing to the crowd in the gallery. I waited tensely for Troax to make his reply. But when he was ordered to do so he said nothing. Simply met the forbidding stares of his judges with a polite smile and shook his head. As I said, he was learning.

Not that he had a chance of persuading them. They obviously had a vested interest in the fortune-teller's booth – one of the many street stalls paying a licence fee to the Council – and nothing perverts the course of justice more surely than money. The upshot was they threw the book at the two of them.

'You men have come uninvited to our city and abused our hospitality,' the chief magistrate said, pompously self-righteous. 'For that you will go to prison for three months.' He glanced up at the gallery and added, 'After you have been flogged.'

They were taken out into the square, stripped to the waist, trussed up to the railings in front of the City Hall and publicly flogged. The sergeant-at-arms was a burly, big-shouldered man and by the time he had finished with them they were unconscious, held upright only by the thongs round their wrists. Hospital cases in dire need of treatment: oxygen masks, blood transfusions, sterile dressings. But there was no ambulance to take them to Casualty. Only a police van and a cell in the city jail.

It looked as though Troax's bold venture into Greece was over before it had begun. No doubt Ferris would be relieved. But my medical conscience was troubled. Silas had the physique to withstand the cruelty of the whip. Troax, small and thin, was much more vulnerable. I went back to the Consulate, changed into uniform and took a taxi to the jail.

When I told the prison governor I had come to inspect the premises with a view to using them for military prisoners en route to Rome and a court martial, he fell over himself to oblige and took me straight down to the high-security cells. They were deep underground, dark and cold, unfit for animals, let alone people. He drew my attention to the massive locks on the iron doors, the thick stone walls, the alarm system; enthusiastic as an estate agent extolling the splendours of a grandiose villa.

'It'll be deserters and the like you have in mind, Colonel?' he said fawningly.

I nodded, masking my disgust. 'Something like that.'

'They'll not get out of here in a hurry, sir. You can depend on that.'

I had a look at Troax and Silas through the spy-hole in the door of their cell and felt my gorge rise. They were slumped half-conscious on verminous straw pallets, covered in blood, their clothes in tatters, their backs like flayed beef. In the dim light of the low-wattage bulb their faces were haggard, ashen with shock, their eyes sunk deep into their heads. I saw that they were manacled; handcuffs linked by chains to leg irons. 'Why the fetters?' I said angrily.

'Regulations, sir.' The governor smiled proudly; a man who would obey any rule, however inhuman.

'For God's sake, look at the state they're in, man. Have you had a doctor in to check them over?'

He shook his head. 'They're not entitled to medical attention. I'm running a prison here, Colonel, not a convalescent home.'

I looked at his plump, eager-to-please face, the small, sly eyes and realized he was telling me what he thought I wanted to hear. But they were in a bad way. Silas would probably recover but I doubted Troax would last another twenty-four hours if left untreated, much less three months. Something had to be done and quickly if he were not to die. And dying was not on the agenda. The last thing Ferris wanted was a martyr hero to light the fuse of revolt. Another Michaelides, another Davidson.

I went back to the City Hall and pulled rank on the Town Clerk who took me in to see the mayor.

He received me with wary cordiality; a silver-haired, weak-faced man with evasive eyes and an overweening sense of his own importance. He took note of my uniform, offered me a chair and asked how he could be of service.

I was in no mood for pleasantries and said bluntly, 'Two men were publicly flogged in the square this afternoon.'

'Two *Jews*, yes.' He picked up a document from his desk. 'I have the magistrates' report here. Vagrant troublemakers from Turkey. We have a short way with their kind in Philippi.'

'So I observed.' I let my disgust show.

He bridled. 'We're on the edge of things here, Colonel. Vulnerable to political infiltrators from the east. We may be only an outpost of the Empire but we know where our duty lies.'

'Restoring the sanity of an emotionally disturbed girl cruelly exploited by her masters is hardly a political act, I think.'

He looked at me, his eyes cunning. 'Unless it's a means to an end. A trick performed in public to unsettle the people.'

'Is that what you think it was?'

He shrugged. 'We can't be too careful. These things have a way of escalating. Call for swift, decisive action.'

'Like a public flogging?'

'Precisely.' He gave me a self-satisfied smile. 'Unpleasant, of course, but it impresses the people wonderfully. Reassures them of our authority and therefore their security.'

I said, deliberately casually, 'You know, I take it, that one of those men you had flogged today is a Roman citizen?'

His eyes flickered. 'What?'

'Two Jews, you said. But one of them – Paul Troax – is also a free-born Roman.' I raised my eyebrows. 'Are you in the habit of flogging Romans in Philippi?'

He licked his lips nervously. 'Well, no. Certainly not. But...'

'And throwing them into jail?'

He stared at me miserably. 'I – I'd no idea Troax was...'

'And didn't take the trouble to find out? Not you nor your magistrates?' I shook my head slowly, letting him sweat a little. 'That was not very wise, Mr Mayor.'

'I can only apologize, Colonel. An unfortunate oversight and much regretted.'

'You can do more than that. I want those men released and taken to hospital.'

'Yes. Yes, of course.' He looked at his watch. 'I'll see to it first thing in the morning.'

'No,' I said sharply. '*I'll* see to it now. Write me a release order for the two of them. Troax and his servant.'

'It'll have to be witnessed by the chief magistrate, I'm afraid, and...'

'Don't stall me, man. If you want to stay mayor, act like one. The Senate doesn't look favourably on inefficient public servants.'

He reached for the phone. 'I'll instruct my clerk to draft it.'

'You'll draft it yourself. Now.'

He slumped in his chair, deflated, and wrote out the order. Signed it with his mayoral seal and handed it to me with a trembling hand.

'I'll need a car.'

'Of course, Colonel. No problem.' He spoke briefly into the phone, cradled the receiver and said, 'All arranged. I – I hope they will quickly recover from their injuries.'

'So do I,' I said levelly. 'For your sake.'

The prison governor read the release order and nodded. 'All correct, sir.' There was something different about him; a sort of suppressed excitement, of new-found confidence. He was respectful but no longer fawning. Nor, oddly enough, surprised.

'They're all right, are they?'

'I think you'll find them much improved, Colonel. This way, if you please.'

Instead of going down to the underground cells he took me upstairs and through a door into his private quarters. There I found Troax and Silas sitting at a table eating a savoury dish of meat and vegetables with fresh-baked bread and a bottle of wine. They had been given baths, bandages, decent clothes. I looked at them, amazed. Troax was obviously still very sore and stiff but his eyes were bright and he had a good colour. Silas was tucking into his food with relish, watched over by the governor's wife and children.

I stepped back into the hall and closed the door. 'I see you've had a change of heart, Governor.'

'It was the singing, Colonel.' He grinned. 'We don't get a lot of that in here as a rule.'

'You mean they were singing?' I said incredulously.

'They were indeed.' The governor went on to describe how he had gone down and found them sitting in the cell singing Jewish psalms. Oozing blood, crawling with lice, shivering with cold and singing their hearts out. And that was not all. The cell door was unlocked and open, the fetters thrown aside. In fact, every cell was open. All the prisoners were free from their chains, could have walked out any time they liked. 'I roused my staff and got the place made secure again. My duty, y'see, sir. We've got murderers in here. Bandits, fire freaks, rapists. And, in any case, a mass escape would've cost me...'

'Your life?' I nodded. 'But these two you favoured. Why?'

'It was the least I could do, sir. A bath, dressings for their wounds, something to eat. They warned me of what had happened. With their singing. All the others were asleep. Didn't know they were free to go. I wouldn't have known either but for the singing.' He smiled. 'One good turn and all that.'

'But who unlocked the cells, struck off the chains?'

'Paul Troax says it was God's doing, sir.'

'Ah. He's been talking to you, has he?'

'Oh, yes. He's been talking.'

Typically, Troax had seized the opportunity to say his piece. And, perhaps because the governor was grateful and also a little afraid of him, he and his family had accepted baptism into the Christian religion.

'He's a remarkable man, Colonel,' the governor said, half-defiant, half-apologetic. Not over-burdened with intelligence, he had been easy game for Troax.

'Yes. Remarkable.'

We went back into the room and they had finished their meal. Troax recognized me but was tactful enough not to show it. I think, looking back, we were both aware that night of a relationship of some kind growing between us. Something of value we were not yet ready to bring out into the open. I was the big fish in the little pond of his followers and he was determined to take his time to land me.

'Good news, gentlemen.' The governor put the release order on the table with a flourish. 'Thanks to the good offices of the Colonel here, you're both pardoned and free to leave whenever you like.'

Troax read the order, looked up and blew his top. 'No,' he said and thumped his fist on the table. 'We were unjustly flogged for a crime we had not committed. Locked up like common criminals and left to rot. And now they want us to sneak out with our tails between our legs?' He shook his head fiercely. 'It won't do. It won't do at all. We're not budging from this place until the mayor comes down in person and makes a full apology and invites us to leave at our own convenience. Then we'll go. Not before.'

The governor paled. 'Please, Sir, don't make trouble for me, nor for yourselves. The Colonel has obtained a free pardon for you both. At considerable personal inconvenience. And...'

'I'm not ungrateful to him, nor to you and your household for the kindness you've shown us. But we don't need a pardon, having committed no offence. What we need – demand – is an apology. And until we get it we're staying put. Back in the cell if necessary.'

I took the governor outside again and asked him where the phone was.

'You're not going to call the mayor at this hour, sir?' he said anxiously. 'It's close to midnight and...'

'Why not?'

'With respect, sir, I wouldn't advise it. The release order can be rescinded, you know.'

'I don't think so. Troax is a Roman citizen.'

He watched me, stunned, as I dialled the number.

The mayor sounded sleepy, indignant and, finally, scared to death. He got the chief magistrate out of bed and the two of them bowed and scraped to Troax with profuse apologies and offers of compensation. Troax heard them out, stony-faced, accepted their apology frigidly, declined any compensation and dismissed them. They went away humiliated. As they were leaving, Troax fired his last shot. 'Should you be contemplating any face-saving disciplinary action against the governor of this prison and his family,' he said icily, 'forget it. The

Colonel will witness to the man's integrity and devotion to duty and he has the ear of some very influential people in Rome. Need I say more?'

The mayor assured him he need not.

'Was I too hard on them, Michael?' Troax said, remembering.

'Not half as hard as they were on you and Silas.'

'I suppose not.' He grinned. 'I rather enjoyed it, y'know. Making them eat humble pie.'

'No more than they deserved.'

He shook his head. 'That was never the Master's way and ought not to be ours. We're called to forgive our enemies, not make them look small.'

'Even he could be scathing sometimes.'

'Yes. Hating the sin, loving the sinners. John Zebedee understood that better than any of us. Though even he has never really forgiven the Sanhedrin for delivering the Master to Pilate.'

'Have you?'

'It's different for me, Michael. I've fought on both sides, remember.' He fell silent, hunched on the bed as if under a great burden. 'I have this vision,' he said then, 'that one day my people – the Jews – will come into the Faith, accepting his forgiveness as I have, to find new life in him.'

'Many of them have.' Jewish families who had defied the anger of the rabbis and given him hospitality and support.

'No. Only a few. I've had more success with the pagans than with Israel's sons and daughters. I've always hoped the Church would be based in Jerusalem. Jewish Christians taking pride of place. But now...' He sighed.

'We're pioneers of a world Faith. And Rome is the centre of that world.'

It was what he had worked for over the years but I heard the wistfulness in that sigh and knew he still clung to the old messianic dream in which all the nations on earth looked to Israel as their religious centre.

'I'm a man at odds with himself, Michael. In Jerusalem I'm a Roman, eager for expansion. In Rome I'm a Jew, lonely and far from home.'

In a lesser man his words would have been self-pitying but I knew him too well. His sadness was not for himself but for those little churches he had founded and to which he now wrote his letters. Letters which Ferris had intercepted and analyzed, believing them to be coded messages fostering revolution against the State. In fact, they were the first attempt to interpret the life and teaching of Jesus Davidson to the pagan world. They would never, perhaps, have the authority of the eyewitness accounts written by the men who had been his closest friends, but they had an authority of their own, giving hope and determination to ordinary men and women trying to work out the implications of the Kingdom in their day-to-day lives.

'They never expected it to be like this, y'know,' he said. 'Peter and John and the others. They were convinced that the world as we know it would come to an end within a few years of the Resurrection and the Kingdom be openly established. All they were concerned about was to tell as many people as possible to prepare for the Apocalypse while there was still time. But how to actually live in the Kingdom now – they'd nothing constructive to say about that.'

'Reject your old ways and believe the good news of

God?' I said. 'As you yourself did in Kohbar's house in Damascus.'

'But that's only the beginning. A declaration of your intent to live out your belief under human governments, human laws. The Kingdom is not of this world but it is *in* this world. The ultimate secret of life.' The old excitement was back in his voice now, impassioned, urgent. As if the cramped little room were a city square and I an audience of hundreds. 'We're creatures of time and place, trapped in history, destined for eternity. But eternity is not something to look forward to after history. Eternity is the ever-present Now. That's what the Master came to show us. He was in time but also outside it. His body died some thirty years ago but his spirit never died. The spirit which healed lepers and cripples, opened blind eyes, brought Lazarus back from his grave. That is what entered into us that Shevuoth, fifty days after the Resurrection, when Peter defied the priests in the Temple court and astounded the crowd of pilgrims there. The miracles we perform are the work of his spirit within us, signs of the present reality of the Kingdom.'

I smiled a little sadly. This was what I had heard him say so often and in so many places, the words tumbling out of his mouth, his good eye shining. It was all so obvious to him, so undeniable. I thought of the years he had spent locked away in this garret, deprived of an audience. And was grieved by the waste of it all.

'I'm not concerned with the end of history,' he said. 'As I continually tell my churches in my letters, what matters is now. What we do with our lives, how we order them to the glory of God. Every day a new beginning, every night a reprieve. We can't just stand about on street corners waiting for time to come to an end. We have to make our faith work here and now.'

This was the secret of his astonishing energy, his disregard for physical pain, his ability to bounce back. Listening to him I could almost share it. But the knowledge of what I was to do tomorrow was a barrier between us. 'Whatever happened to that girl in Philippi?' I said, for something to say.

'What?' He blinked as if waking from a dream. 'Oh, we fixed up for her to stay with a Christian family. I forget their name but they took her into their home with love.' He smiled. 'Pretty little thing when they'd washed her face and given her something decent to wear.' He shook his head. 'There've been so many scattered halfway round the world. Impossible to keep track of them all.'

I nodded. It was the same with my patients. Some I remembered, some I forgot. Usually the ones I'd been able to help. It was the failures I remembered.

As if reading my thoughts, he said, 'Something I can't forget is Athens, Michael. I only wish I could.'

6

'Just run that past me again, Lucas,' Ferris said, suddenly very alert.

We were speaking over a secure line from 21 Army Group HQ, Berea, to his office in Rome. I told him again that Troax had established new churches in Thessalonica and Berea. Both small. Both a mix of Jews and pagans. In each town there had been trouble. The magistrates brought in. Heavy fines imposed.

'Yes, yes. But on what charge?' he said impatiently.

'Disturbing the peace. In particular, encouraging people to call Jesus Davidson their king and renounce their allegiance to the Emperor.'

'Renounce their allegiance to the Emperor. That's what I've been waiting to hear. That's treason, Lucas. The proof I've been looking for.' He chuckled grimly. 'It's out in the open at last.'

'Hardly that, sir. The fines have been paid. The case closed.'

'Don't you believe it, Lucas. This is only the beginning, the first glimpse of the true political thrust behind the curtain of religion. Where is Troax now?'

'Still here. Keeping a low profile. He needs a rest after that hammering he took in Philippi.'

'Until his urban guerrillas sprang him out of jail.' It was what I had implied in a coded fax, knowing Ferris would reject any suggestion of divine intervention. 'Is his minder still with him?'

'Silas? Yes, he's here with Timothy.'

'Oh, the Greek's turned up, has he?'

'Yes.' The boy's arrival in Thessalonica had done much to cheer and comfort Troax.

'There you are, then. They're up to something. Have to be, for God's sake.'

Le mot juste, I thought. 'Very possibly, sir.'

'You can bet on it, Lucas. They've got the ball rolling and they won't stop it now. Stay with it, Mike.' He only called me Mike when he was pleased with my news. 'The moment Troax makes a move – any move – I want to know.'

'I'll keep you posted, sir.'

'Do that. And congratulations,' he said and rang off.

A week later Troax was on the train for Athens. I watched him board it, travelling second class, seen off by Silas and Timothy. He was still walking a little stiffly after that vicious flogging in Philippi and some of the bounce had gone out of him. But his head was up, his eyes bright, anticipating the capital and all the opportunities it offered. Opportunities he wanted for himself initially, not to be shared with the other two. He'd lit a torch in Greece and was set to carry it to Athens and set the city alight.

I took my seat in a first class sleeper as befitted my rank and tried not to worry about him. I was still not convinced that Ferris was right. Still saw the little Jew as a religious prophet not a political agitator. But if he did in Athens what he had done here in the north he was heading for real trouble. On the surface, relations between Athens and Rome were cordial. But the Greeks still considered themselves a superior race, the founders of European civilization, the real brains behind the might of Rome. They paid lip-service to the Emperor but had little affection for him. A movement which offered a greater, universal King would find many sympathizers among them, its ambassador made welcome. Religiously and politically Athens was a major prize. A rich vein of power waiting to be tapped. Could Troax tap it? More to the point, could he control it when it was tapped?

Athens is a great place for talking. Intellectual debates by scholars (thick on the ground there) which spill over into the conversation in the smart cafés which are so much a part of the city's life; a city in which philosophers talk like poets and bankers talk like philosophers. It all makes for a leisurely – almost indolent – life in which the buying of a loaf of bread becomes an act of deep, enigmatic significance.

Sitting in the glass-and-marble splendour of a bar on the morning of my third day there I discovered the word was that a new teacher had come to the ghetto and was vigorously attacking the worship of idols and pouring scorn on the ancient gods of Olympus. Whilst this had gone down well in the synagogue it was unlikely to appeal to the Greeks. Not that they still believed in those mythical divinities with human passions and questionable morality, but they were jealous of the hundreds of statues to them for which Athens is famous, and quick to take offence if they were ridiculed. Especially by a foreigner. Especially if he was a Jew. It was not a matter of religion so much as of civic pride. Bad manners rather than heresy.

I smiled ruefully to myself. Troax had put his finger unerringly on a sensitive nerve. Which meant he was back on form.

The man at the next table, silver-haired, impeccably

groomed, said to his companion in a broad drawl, 'I hear the fellow's going to speak in the market this morning. Worth a stroll round there to hear him, d'you think?'

The elegant girl with him made a face. She was young enough to be his daughter but obviously wasn't. 'If you like,' she said. 'I suppose I can look for a dress this afternoon.'

He smiled lasciviously. 'I have other plans for us this afternoon, my dear.'

'Have you now?' She gave him a teasing look. 'And what might those be?'

He leaned forward, whispering in her ear.

She giggled. 'Now there's a surprise.'

I paid my bill and set off through the fashionable streets lined with public buildings of classical beauty. Lined with superb statues, too, much sought after by wealthy Romans to grace their villas. I found them marvellously beautiful but knew Troax would hate them, every one a blasphemous insult to his God.

The market at the foot of the Acropolis was the social centre of the city's life; an intriguing mix of the intellectual and the commercial. There was no way Troax could resist it. He had done his statutory duty in the synagogue. Now it was time to take on the Greeks.

He had found himself a platform on a flight of marble steps and had gathered a small crowd. Athenians have always been connoisseurs of oratory, as interested in the speaker's style and appearance as in the content of his message. I wondered how they would react to his aggressive approach and was a little worried. I need not have been. He had taken their measure and tailored his words accordingly, speaking clearly but calmly. None of the passion, none of the fire. This was a Troax I had never heard before, delivering an innocuous little speech in praise of Greek culture. A schoolboy essay on its ancient glories, its remarkable contribution to the world of learning. The crowd loved it, nodding in approval, pleasantly surprised to hear such anodyne flattery.

'He's good,' a man beside me said, 'for a Jew.'

His companion nodded. 'For a Jew he's brilliant.'

You're up to something, I thought as the soothing words floated over me. This isn't why you've come to Athens. This is a ploy to get yourself accepted, listened to, admired.

And so it proved. As he came to his peroration, bowing to their applause, two men met him at the foot of the steps. Two scholars. There was no mistaking that. They spoke to him quietly and he nodded, fell into step beside them and walked away, a spring in his legs, a smile in his eyes. As if that sugary speech had been a triumph.

I followed at a discreet distance as they crossed the city towards the Areopagus. It was then I realized what he was about.

That speech had been deliberately flattering. A calculated eulogy designed to get himself into the Areopagus in front of the cream of Athenian society – the scholars, the magistrates, the men of distinction and influence. The kind of audience he had always wanted.

I settled in a seat near the back of the auditorium as Troax was courteously introduced and invited to address the assembly. He mounted the rostrum and stood in silence for a moment or two, breathing deeply, settling his mind; an insignificant figure in secondhand clothes with nothing to commend him but his courage, his passion and his monumental ego. I was aware of the men around me nudging each other with amused smiles and felt my heart sink. They had brought him here to make sport of him, all his carefully calculated plans turned against him. He was so obviously out of his depth. A street orator with nothing to say to such an august company.

But his opening sentence gripped them in a velvet glove.

'Gentlemen of Athens,' he said with a little bow, his voice deep and calm his eyes confident. 'I am grateful indeed to have this opportunity to address so distinguished, so world-famous an assembly. Thank you for your gracious hospitality.'

And it wasn't just flattery. He meant every word, his sincerity transparently genuine.

'I see that in every way you Athenians are deeply religious, your glorious city graced by so many beautiful places of worship. Why, you even have a shrine dedicated to the Unknown God. That is very much to your credit and I applaud you for it...'

I saw heads turning, nodding in pleased surprise. This man was nothing to look at but he spoke like an angel.

'It is this Unknown God of whom I wish to speak to you today for he is known to me and I am his messenger...' And he was up and running down the familiar track which led us back to the carpenter's workshop in Nazareth and a young man called Jeshua ('Or, as you would say, Jesus') sent from God to bring good news of forgiveness and hope to the world. 'To the world, gentlemen. He was a Jew of royal blood, a true son of David our greatest king. Yet his message is a universal one, as relevant here in Athens – and indeed in Rome – as it is in Jerusalem...' And now he was immensely impressive, speaking from his heart with compelling power so that he seemed to grow in stature before us all, the ugliness of his face softened by a kind of radiance. The passion was back in his voice but controlled without anger.

The room was still, his listeners caught up in the drama of it. I felt a rising excitement as he took us through the years of miracle and grace, the admiring crowds, the discomfited priests, to the tragedy of betrayal in the dark garden, the rigged trial before the Sanhedrin, the ritual flogging, the confrontation with Pilate. This was a variation on the classical Greek drama and the audience listened with mounting approval, some of them in tears as he took us through the final journey through the bitter streets, the weeping women, the jeering rabbis, to the cross waiting on the unforgiving hill. The agony of the nails, the thirst, the tortured lungs, the flies. The last despairing cry. The undignified rush to finish it before the Passover. The hurried burial in another man's tomb.

I had heard it all many times but never told with greater impact. The Athenians were spellbound, caught up in the horror of it and the pain and the injustice.

'The Unknown, Unrecognized God who came to give us life and was himself brutally murdered,' he said. 'This is the God I bring to you today if you will open your hearts and minds to receive him. Jesus the Christ, the Son of God, the King of kings.'

If he had stopped there. Given them time to think about it, discuss it among themselves. If he had done that. Planted the seed in their minds and let it take root, leaving the end of the story until a later date... But he didn't.

'You will think it strange indeed,' he said, 'that I bring

you a dead God. Strange and terrible. The triumph of evil over good.'

I knew what was coming next and squirmed in my seat as his head came up high. 'But the story doesn't end there in defeat and death. Three days after he was buried he rose again, breaking out of the tomb in majesty and power, appearing to his friends. He was dead and is alive again, a man no longer but the living spirit of God himself infusing them with power, sharing their lives as he dwells in them. Opening the Kingdom of Heaven to all who believe in him. Men of Athens, this Jesus is the Christ who...' His voice faltered in shocked disbelief as his audience began to get up and walk out, shaking their heads, smiling behind their hands. He stared at them open-mouthed. In his experience people attacked him, arrested him, abused him. What they didn't do was ignore him.

He spread his arms wide in a desperate plea for them to stay. 'No. Please. Listen to me. I...' But he had lost them with that statement of a resurrection.

I saw the misery in his face, his eyes puzzled, his shoulders slumped; outward indications of a terrible mental struggle. Anxious for his sanity, I pushed my way down towards the rostrum. He needed a friend with understanding. One of the leading scholars touched his arm in gentle reproof. 'A god disguised as a man, yes,' he said. 'Our own religion tells us that the gods come often in disguise to share our troubles. But a dead man raised from his tomb?' He shook his head. 'I'm sorry. Religion and logic go hand-in-hand. We worship the gods with our intellect, looking to them for the reason of life. The common people have their statues and their little rituals. But we have our minds to think about the gods and so grow to be like them. But there's no logical explanation for a dead man brought back to life. That makes no sense at all.'

'You are wrong, sir,' Troax said tiredly, making a last effort to get through to him. 'If he truly is God – and he is – it's the only logical end to his story. The only thing that does make sense. Only God can defeat death.'

The scholar shrugged politely. 'An interesting idea if a rather improbable one. You must come again sometime, Paul Troax, and we will hear more of this matter.'

'So he blew it?' Ferris said over the phone that night.

'One word too many and he lost them.' With the backing of the Areopagus pundits Athens could have been his. I remembered the old saying: 'What Athens thinks today, Rome does tomorrow.' He had come to the cradle of European civilization and so nearly won it over. And was now discredited.

'Will he go back for another try?'

'No.' The wound too deep, the disappointment too bitter.

'Extraordinary,' Ferris said. 'Shot his bolt, then?'

'In Athens, yes.' Perhaps it had been too much to hope for, to go for the capital first and conquer it. Even Jesus Davidson had taken three years to do that.

'What's that supposed to mean, Lucas. He's pulled out, surely?'

'Going tomorrow,' I said. Unnoticed, already forgotten. Not even the satisfaction of a trial. Slinking away with his tail between his legs.

'Where to?'

'Corinth,' I said. Perhaps he couldn't face Silas and Timothy; not until he'd sorted himself out.

'Is he, by God?' Ferris said interestedly.

I knew why. Corinth was a hot bed of intrigue and political unrest, the streets swarming with a volatile mix of nationalities. Greeks, Turks, Arabs, Egyptians, Romanians washed up by the tide. A town of great wealth (most of it dishonestly gained) and grinding poverty. Of smugglers and drug dealers, gun-runners, pimps and prostitutes. A port where arguments were settled with a knife or a bullet, where corruption was rife, gang-wars commonplace, the law openly ridiculed. Exactly the sort of environment Troax would thrive on. If he were to get a foothold in Europe it would be there.

'Stay with him, Lucas. I've got a hunch we'll find the sort of political evidence we need this time.'

'I can't go this week, sir. I'm chairing a medical conference in the hospital at Piraeus. If I back out now my cover will be blown.'

'Understood. But don't leave it too long.'

In the event it was ten days before I could get away but I need not have worried. Troax stayed in Corinth eighteen months.

'Corinth?' Porteous said, a gleam in his beery eyes.

I nodded. It was my last night in Piraeus and I was enjoying a quiet brandy with a couple of my medical colleagues in the mess after dinner.

'Spot of leave, is it?' Porteous said, sitting down uninvited, a pewter tankard of porter in his hand. 'You trick cyclists've got it made. Always swanning off to the bright lights and the loose women while hard-working types like me soldier on.'

'You're breaking my heart,' I said. He was the Senior

Equipment Officer for our hospitals in Greece; a bluff, hard-drinking man nobody loved. A civilian in uniform with a massive inferiority complex and the manners of a warehouse foreman. 'We all have our problems, y'know.'

'And you cash in on 'em.' He gulped down some beer, wiped his mouth with the back of his hand. 'Well, as you're going there anyway, you could do something useful for a change. We've got a biggish contract for tents for field hospitals with a firm in Corinth. Reliable enough usually, for civilians, but they're way behind schedule on this one. Probably diverting some of the output to other customers to make a quick profit. Cash on the nail and no tax. If you could do a bit of chasing for me?' He scribbled the address and contract number on a slip of paper and handed it to me. 'The owner's called Aquila Nikolas. Jewish, of course. A personal appearance'll impress him far more than half-a-dozen phone calls. Turn up in uniform and lean on him, eh?'

Slightly piqued by his assumption that I would be his errand boy, I said, 'If it's so urgent why don't you go yourself?'

He looked at me with genuine surprise. 'Me? With my workload? You must be joking. I've more than enough to do here without taking time out to chivvy a bunch of Jews,' he said, implying that I hadn't.

'My dear chap,' I said. 'I'd no idea you were so snowed under.'

He glared round the table. 'You medical types. You've no idea what a real job's like, have you? Take his pulse, Sister. Empty his bed-pan, nurse. A ten-minute walk round the wards every morning and the rest of the day your own.'

'OK,' I said, 'you've made your point.' I pocketed the paper. At least it gave me a valid reason for visiting the back streets of Corinth not normally frequented by tourists.

The next morning I cadged a ride with a couple of junior officers going on leave. High-spirited young lieutenants as dashing as the sleek Alfa convertible they drove. The road was winding, full of blind corners, and they enlivened the journey by taking turns at the wheel to see who could drive the furthest without using the brakes. They made me feel old.

I showed my CI card at the Consulate. As always, Ferris's signature opened all doors and I was given a pleasant third-floor room with a view over the bay. The following day I took a cab to the industrial area near the docks, located the factory and went inside. My uniform had the same effect there as my card at the Consulate.

Nikolas received me in his office above the factory floor. He was in his early fifties, dark of hair and eyes, with a firm handshake and a courteous but not obsequious manner. A king in his modest kingdom. He gave me coffee and asked how he could be of service, obviously scenting a contract.

I disillusioned him. 'What about the contract you already have with Major Porteous in Piraeus? Two weeks overdue, I believe?'

'Ah, yes, Colonel. I apologize for the delay. Half my workers have been down with a virus and are only now beginning to come back to work.'

'Your problem, not mine.'

'Indeed. But we're on top of it now. Expect to complete within the next few days.'

'At a discount, presumably?'

'Of course. With us our customers come first. Especially our military clients.'

'Ten per cent?'

He smiled. 'Five. Even then we'll barely cover our costs.'

I nodded. 'By the end of this week?'

'Certainly, Colonel.'

'And you'll ring Major Porteous to that effect? Today?'

He said he would.

I held out my hand. 'A pleasure to do business with you, Mr Nikolas.' Which was more than Porteous would have said. But I liked the man's brisk honesty.

We were walking back across the factory floor when I spotted Troax. He was bending over the big cutting-table, the shears nimble in his hand. He didn't look up as we passed. At the door my cab was waiting. 'That man on the cutting-table seems to know what he's about.'

'Troax?' Nikolas nodded. 'Oh, he's good. The best there is. Does the work of three men. I wish he was on my permanent staff. He was just passing through with a bit of time on his hands and offered to pitch in. Quite a character. Knocked about the world a bit and has a fund of stories to tell. Typical Turk, of course. Talk your head off given half a chance.'

'He's not by any chance one of the Tarsus Troaxes?'

'Yes. Used to run his father's factory there. Why? D'you know him?'

'I know of him. I do a fair bit of travelling myself for the army and our paths have crossed once or twice.'

'An interesting man, sir.'

'Yes. So what went wrong?'

'Wrong?' Nikolas said, suddenly wary.

'A skilled tent-maker, heir to his father's business, which also has contracts with the Forces. And he turns up here to work on the factory floor. There must be a reason.'

'Well, sir, I...'

'He's not political, is he? A troublemaker? One of these union activists who think the workers should be running the country?'

Nikolas hesitated. 'I shouldn't think so. He's working just for his keep. Seems totally disinterested in money. That's not like a union man.'

'No. He's staying with you is he?'

'Yes. Least we could do. He's had a hard time of it lately. Doesn't talk about it much but reading between the lines I get the feeling he's a bit – well – bruised in spirit, if you know what I mean? We're both rather worried about him, my wife and I.'

'Oh?'

Nikolas hesitated again. 'Look, Colonel, I don't want to impose on you but you're a doctor. I wonder if you'd care to come to supper with us this evening? I'd appreciate your professional opinion about him.'

I smiled. 'That's very civil of you, Mr Nikolas. I'd be happy to come. Thank you.'

I rode back to the Consulate in a thoughtful mood. Troax might well just be doing a friend a favour; covering his tracks by merging into the background. But I remembered Nikolas' hesitation, his obvious anxiety about Troax. 'Not like a union man,' he had said. Was this a hint that Troax was planning to create unrest in the unions? The first step towards a strike? A political coup to swing the workers behind him?

'In this job, Lucas,' Ferris had said to me once, 'we get results with a mixture of dogged persistence and good luck.' I began to wonder if my luck was about to turn. A prospect which both cheered and depressed me.

There were just the four of us at supper: Nikolas and Priscilla, his wife, Troax and I. His eyes narrowed a little when I walked in but he greeted me civilly enough. The meal was simple but good; some excellent fish, vegetables in a piquant sauce, a fresh fruit salad, chilled white wine. But Troax ate with little appetite and was unusually subdued. I guessed he was still smarting over his failure in the Areopagus. He was not one to take defeat lightly. Few public speakers are.

Nikolas was a generous host and drew me into the conversation easily, interested in my medical work, asking intelligent questions. He was remarkably well-read for his social status and had a quick, receptive mind. Troax said very little but I caught him watching me once or twice with speculative eyes. Probably wondering why I kept turning up wherever he happened to be. I wasn't sure how much the Nikolases knew about his religious activities and was careful not to mention them. Once he realized this he was more at ease in a morose sort of way. Loss of appetite, tiredness, a sort of brooding melancholy. All symptoms of an incipient nervous breakdown.

After supper, as I was preparing to take my leave, Troax said, 'Where are you staying, Colonel?'

I told him. Nikolas suggested calling for a cab for me. I said I fancied a walk before turning in.

It was a cue for Troax and he responded quickly. 'Mind if I come with you some of the way?' he said casually.

But I saw the plea in his eyes and nodded. 'Be glad of your company, Mr Troax.'

I suppose we made an odd couple; the small, shabby Jew and the long-striding officer in uniform, pacing the dimly lit streets towards the bright lights of the city centre. The night air was pleasantly cool with the salt smell of the sea in it and there were few people about. We walked in silence for a while and then he said abruptly with something of his old aggression, 'Why are you following me, Lucas? Cyprus, Lystra, Philippi, Athens and now Corinth. Why?'

I shrugged. 'Coincidence. We're both travelling men and it's a small world. You serve your God. I serve the Emperor, visiting military hospitals. We're both healers. You heal with a power I don't begin to understand. I heal – or try to – using psychiatric techniques.'

'Which I don't understand.'

'And don't need to. Yours is a far greater gift than mine.'

He looked up at me with a flash of his old excitement. 'It could be yours, too.'

'If I believed in your God?'

'My God and yours. The one and only God, the Father of us all.'

'Perhaps.' We fell silent again for a moment or two. 'Now it's my turn to be curious,' I said then. 'What're you really trying to do? You're not just a healer. You're also an orator. The healing's only a small part of what you do. Impressive. Eminently worthwhile. But not important in itself. It's what you talk about that matters, isn't it?'

'You understand that?' he said, pleased.

'Oh, yes. What I don't understand is where it's all

going. On the face of it you're a religious man. A prophet, I suppose. But it's a religion without a temple, without priests. A religion of the streets, for the poor and oppressed who live out their wretched lives in the gutter. You try to graft it on to your Jewish faith – with little success, I gather – but it doesn't work in the synagogues. Nor, if you'll forgive me saying so, in the Areopagus.'

He winced. 'I saw you there.'

'A good try. But it didn't come off.'

'I tried to do too much too soon.'

'And very nearly succeeded. Might well have done if you hadn't moved from logic, when you had them interested, to the impossible, when you lost them. I mean, resurrection from the dead!' I shook my head. 'You might get away with that among ignorant, superstitious people in deep distress, willing to grasp at any straw. But you can't expect intelligent men to swallow that.'

'But it's true. Verified by eyewitnesses whose lives have been transformed by it.'

'And you believe them?'

He stopped and faced me. 'You ask me that? You were there in Damascus when he opened my eyes and set me free. What further proof d'you want?'

I said carefully, 'That's proof of your own belief. I respect that. Envy it as a psychologist fascinated by the mystery of the human mind. But as proof of a resurrection? I can't accept that. The whole idea is too fanciful, too bizarre. And too dangerous.'

'Dangerous?'

'What you're saying in those speeches of yours is not just religious. It's politically explosive. You talk about a kingdom greater and more powerful than Rome, ruled by a king who is greater than Caesar.'

'Yes,' he said firmly. 'Yes.'

'How can that be? Your king was a carpenter in a small town nobody outside Israel's ever heard of. He set himself up against his own religion and against Rome. Not just a prophet, albeit a heretical one, but also a revolutionary. Your own people condemned him as a blasphemer. Pilate condemned him as a traitor.'

'He hated poverty and loved the poor, healed the sick and fed the hungry and...'

'Is dead. Dead and buried, leaving a legacy of public disturbances, innocent people suffering, their lives turned upside down, their children victimized, their wives dishonoured. Is this the freedom he promised them? Is this the kingdom of your God?'

'You don't understand. He...'

'No,' I said. 'But I understand this. While he was alive they followed him eagerly. Risked their homes, their jobs, their lives for him. But who will take those risks for a ghost? For a memory already fading? For a cause already lost?'

'Is that what you think?' he said hotly.

'It's what I know.'

'Do you?' And now the force was back in his voice, his eyes bright in the street lamps. 'Then do you also know that the cause, far from being lost, is growing by the day? From Philippi east across Turkey, in every city, every town I have visited there is now a nucleus of believers taking exactly those risks and growing stronger because of them. Little churches meeting in houses, working together, learning together, celebrating week by week the resurrection of the Master, filled with his spirit, spreading the word.' He took my arm and we began to walk on. 'I failed in Athens,' he said, 'this time. But already, here in Corinth, people are beginning to listen. I'm not popular in the synagogue – although even there some believe and want to know more of the Master. But the city is wide open to me. A fertile field. Soon we'll have a Greek church here, Jew and Gentile reconciled in the Faith.'

There was no stopping him now. We reached the square in front of the Consulate and he was still in full flow, enthusiastic, the words tripping off his tongue. As a doctor I was delighted. Our conversation had cleared his mind, revived his spirit. But as an Intelligence agent I was worried for him. He was talking revolution against the State. There was no doubt of that. But what kind of a revolution would emerge when he had enough churches set in place, enough manpower behind him to make his move? A religious one or a political one? Everything he said could be made to fit either.

I had no doubt which one Ferris would choose to believe.

We shook hands and I watched him start to walk back, a spring in his step, his head high. I was honest enough to acknowledge that I had played a minor part in restoring his confidence. The spirit within him – whatever it was – had done that.

He turned on the corner and raised a hand in salute. Where would we meet again? And in what circumstances?

My fax to Ferris that night was brief. 'Settled in Corinth. Working at his trade on an army contract. Nothing to report.'

7

'You still weren't sure of me in Corinth, were you, Michael?' Troax's voice was amused. 'Afraid I was recruiting a citizen army to rise against Rome.'

'Something like that, yes.' Outside the window the light was beginning to fade now, shadows gathering in the corners of the garret. I heard footsteps on the stairs as the guard was changed.

'That was never on the agenda,' he said. 'An Empire can be won by force but must rule with the willing consent of the people. Co-operation, not oppression. Peace, not tyranny.'

'But the law must be enforced,' I said.

He shook his head impatiently. 'No. It must be accepted by the people, not forced upon them at gunpoint. Laws are made for the people by the people. We must win their consent if we are not to descend into chaos. My intent has always been to avert that disaster. To take the authority out of the hands of a corrupt and frightened government and put it into the hands of Christians. To cleanse the body politic, transforming the State – and eventually the world – with the Spirit of the Master. He alone can rescue us from our follies and give us the lasting peace all people desire but few find.'

'A religious revolution?'

'Of course. What else? Why suffer under a human king when you can live freely under God – the one, the only King?' He leaned forward, his good eye gleaming. 'I believe we're close to doing that, Michael. From Jerusalem, right round the Eastern Mediterranean through Turkey and Greece, we Christians are already a civilizing influence wielding a power far greater than our numbers suggest, strategically placed, well-prepared. And now Peter is here in Rome, waiting in the wings, we have a firm foothold in the capital itself.'

'And Nero,' I said slowly, 'is still on the throne.'

'But not for much longer. The writing is on the wall for him and his toadies.' He was speaking quietly but with immense conviction. 'We've come this far and nothing can stop us now. All I need is a chance to speak for the Master before the Senate.' He grinned ruefully. 'It won't be another Athens, y'know. Four years ago it might have been. Too much too soon. But not now. I'll not make that mistake again.'

Your dream, I thought, or Ferris's nightmare. And felt my throat tighten knowing what Nero had in store for him. To come so far through suffering and disappointment and in the end be denied the fulfilment of his life's work, either in the arena or in exile. Given the choice I was sure he would opt for the former, going out in a blaze of agony in front of the jeering crowd as his Master had done. Better to be sacrificed, his death a triumph, than to wither away anonymous and forgotten on some lonely island.

For one mad moment I toyed with a third option. A needle slipped into his arm by one he trusted, his eyes accusing as he drifted painlessly into death. And knew I couldn't do it.

He smiled. 'Memories, Michael?'

'Good ones,' I said guiltily. He was so honest, so open and so vulnerable.

He dabbed at his weeping eye, wincing at the pain. 'When did you decide about me? And the Master I serve?'

'You know he's my Master now?' I said, surprised.

'Oh yes. I know.'

'I've never told anyone.' A covert Christian avoiding confrontation.

'You didn't have to. In some of us the Spirit is talkative, in others quietly alive. A faith needing no words to explain itself.'

'I can't pinpoint it,' I said truthfully. 'We don't all have an encounter on the Damascus road.'

'No.'

'I suppose it happened gradually over the years,' I said, 'and slowly took root.'

He nodded. 'A seed sown in darkness pushing up towards the light.' It was a metaphor he often used, borrowed from the Master. 'And finding it – where? In Ephesus?'

The early summer of 53 saw the end of a bitter campaign against the wild hill-tribes of Bulgaria. It's bad country up there in the mountains and the Third Legion (the famous Thirsty Third) had a rough time of it before the final battle when they trapped the rebels in a narrow valley and virtually wiped them out.

The week before had brought us horrific scenes on TV when our troops overran a huge prison camp left unguarded in the retreat and its atrocities were uncovered for all the world to see. Inside the wire cages the cream of the Roman army, reduced by brutal ill-treatment and torture to shuffling skeletons covered in sores and festering wounds, stared blankly at their liberators, too emaciated to get up and greet them. The cameras panned slowly over their gaunt, scarred faces, across the compound to the piled corpses rotting

unburied in the filth and the flies, and on to the
relieving troopers standing appalled beside their tanks.
Interviewed in close-up, a tank commander in a voice
choked with anger, 'When we catch up with the
animals that did this there'll be no prisoners taken.
We'll go in with flame-throwers and obliterate the
bastards.'

And so they did.

I was in Troas then, after a stint in an advance dressing-
station at Plodniv, working with a psychiatric team in a
tented hospital outside the town, trying to piece
together broken minds when the surgeons had finished
repairing broken bodies. The suffering was terrible. Our
wards were like an annexe of hell; a bedlam of manic
shrieks and incoherent gibbering as our patients relived
the nightmare of pain and degradation at the hands of
their captors. We were working round the clock and
with only modest success. The worst cases mercifully
died. Of the rest, only a few recovered their sanity. The
majority faced a bleak future in asylums, a danger to
themselves and to others.

When Ferris's signal came through towards the end of
June it was a welcome relief.

Eight months earlier, when our casualties in the field
had begun to escalate, he had reluctantly agreed to
release me temporarily. Troax seemed to have run out of
steam and had settled down in Corinth with the
Nikolases, keeping a low profile. Ferris planted a sleeper
in the factory to inform him if and when Troax got itchy
feet again. Then I would be reactivated.

The signal was typically curt: 'He's in Ephesus. Why?'

Suppressing my feelings of guilt to be leaving my
hard-worked colleagues in Troas, I changed into civvies,

rented a run-of-the-mill Fiat and became a tourist driving south to Ephesus.

I booked into the Imperial Hotel in Silver Street. Not so grand as its name implied, it was a comfortable, three-star establishment in the heart of the city with a cocktail lounge, a large restaurant, en suite rooms and a roof garden. After the tented wards in Troas it was a palace.

I took a long hot shower, put a coded message on Ferris's answering machine to let him know I was in situ and went up to the roof garden for coffee, sitting in the dappled shade of a trellised vine, the muted sound of the traffic in the street below oddly soothing.

'On holiday, are we?' The man at the next table was thick-set and balding, wearing a city suit with a white shirt and a rather off-putting tie, working his way steadily through a plate of baklava; those rich, honey-saturated cakes you only find east of the Aegean, every mouthful a calorific time-bomb.

I nodded politely.

He grinned. 'You look like you need one, brother.' He wiped a blob of honey off his chin with a finger. 'Been over-doing things, have we?' He had a harsh voice and an accent which, like his workman's hands, belied his managerial clothes.

'A bit. I've been up north since last autumn.'

'Oh, ah? Soldiering, like?'

'Reporting,' I said, bending the facts a little.

'War correspondent, eh? Bad as you chaps made it sound was it?'

'Bad enough.' I shrugged. 'Still, it's all over now.'

'We hope. Wars on our doorstep we don't need. Bad for business. Our takings are well down this year.'

'I suppose,' I said tightly, remembering those sobbing, broken men I had left up in Troas.

He swallowed a large bite of cake. 'You wouldn't be interested in a busman's holiday, would you?'

'Not really.'

'Pity. There's a big story waiting here. A scoop for the right man, Mister...?'

'Michaels.'

'I'm Suliman.' He tilted his head expectantly.

'Ah,' I said.

'Doesn't mean anything to you?'

'Should it?'

He grinned. 'Well, let's just say I'm not unknown in the town. I'm the General Secretary of the Federation of Trade Unions incorporating the silversmiths – they're the big boys with most muscle – and allied trades. We're what makes this town tick and those bigwigs on the Council know it.' He pushed his plate away, brushed crumbs off his jacket and sat back. 'Ephesus lives off the tourist industry, see? People come from all over to visit the temple and gawp at the statue of Diana behind the altar. You haven't seen it yet?'

'I just got in today.'

'Oh, ah? Well, it's worth a look if only because of its size. Fifteen feet high and solid stone.' He winked. 'The story is that it fell out of the sky when this was just a village and they built the temple round it, installed the priests and sat back to watch the money roll in. Rubbish, of course. Well, most religion is, isn't it? The sculptors made it – with more enthusiasm than skill, I might say. Horrible-looking thing. Ugly as all get out. More like a monster than a goddess. But the tourists are hooked on it and blow their travellers cheques on souvenirs to take back home. Miniature silver statues, properly mounted and sold in a polished wooden casket. Studded with diamonds too, some of 'em.'

'Fascinating,' I said in a bored voice.

He shook his head, smiling. 'Ah well, I don't suppose it means anything to an educated gentleman like yourself, sir. But we'd be in Queer Street without it. My word, we would. On the wrong side of the Aegean, see? Out in the sticks. Nothing here to match Athens or Corinth. But with Diana rooting for us, we're famous.'

And greedy, I thought, and cynical. I said, 'You mentioned a scoop, Mr Suliman?'

'Aye, I'm coming to that. Just filling you in on the background, like.' He looked round cautiously but apart from a family at a table on the far side of the garden we were alone. 'The fact is, we've got a bit of a crisis looming up.'

'Have you now?' He had this rather tiresome trick of throwing out a sentence and waiting expectantly for a response.

'Financial problems, if you follow me?'

What else? I thought. 'I'm listening.'

'There's a rumour going round that Diana's a fraud. Not a goddess at all. Just a socking great lump of granite displayed in the temple to separate tourists from their money.'

I smiled. 'Well, isn't she?'

'To you and me, perhaps. But that's not the point. If the tourists stop believing in her the bottom'll fall out of the city's economy. Hundreds of skilled craftsmen thrown on the scrap heap. No market for souvenirs, see? Hotels standing empty. Cafés closing right, left and centre. Beggars on every street corner. Robberies, muggings, murders. And that spells ruin, brother. Ruin with a capital R.'

'Ah,' I said, recognizing the rhetoric of a union boss. 'And that's my scoop, is it? When it happens.'

'Oh, it'll happen all right, unless...' He broke off, looking past me, raising his hand. 'Over here, brother.'

I turned my head and saw a man coming out of the lift. Suliman pulled out a chair for him and said quietly, 'Here's your scoop, Mr Michaels.' He introduced the man as Demetrius, president of the SSU (Silversmiths Union). He looked the part. A tall, thin man with pale grey eyes in a lean, aggressive face; wide mouth stretched thinly over large teeth, a cap of dark red hair, an air of truculent defiance.

'Mr Michaels is a reporter,' Suliman said like a conjuror producing a rabbit out of a hat.

Demetrius scowled (he had the face for it). 'I thought this was to be a private meeting. What's he doing here?' he said ungraciously.

'He's here to make you famous, brother. Put this town on the map and solve all our problems.'

'If I'm interested enough,' I said flatly. 'All I've heard so far is speculation based on rumour. Not much of a basis to work on.'

'There will be tomorrow,' Suliman said. 'Tell him, brother.'

Which, after some hesitation and a great deal of reluctance, Demetrius did.

When he had finished, I said, 'Right. As I understand it, this man Troax has been stirring things in the city for the past week. Making subversive speeches about Diana, scaring off the tourists and generally making a nuisance of himself. Yes?'

They nodded.

'And you're beginning to feel threatened by him and have decided to call a meeting of all the union members tomorrow morning and take appropriate action to set Diana back on her pedestal.'

'Fight for our rights,' Demetrius said fiercely, 'while we've still got rights to fight for.'

'Amen to that, brother,' Suliman said heavily.

'And what exactly do you hope to achieve by this?'

Suliman said, 'Well, it's obvious, surely? Get the little Jew arrested and locked up where he can't do any more damage. Give the priests a boost and get things back to normal with a few special offers. Like ten per cent off all souvenirs for a limited period. And vouchers – already printed – for free wine with meals at selected hotels. That's the union way, brother. Generous, customer-friendly, honest.' He gave me a benevolent, man-of-the-people smile. Friendly if not particularly honest. I guessed that when the limited period expired the prices of souvenirs would rise sharply.

'And that's the story you want me to write?'

'In on the ground floor, Mr Michaels. It'll be front-page stuff, y'know. We'll make sure of that.'

'And where's this meeting to be held?'

'In the square outside the temple. Ten o'clock in the morning when everyone's out and about. We'll do it in style. Union banners, placards, a public address system on the temple steps. Demetrius has his speech prepared and will really pull the stops out. We'll have that interfering little Jew up before the bench and behind bars before he knows what's hit him.'

It was a scenario Troax would thrive on. I said, 'A religious man, you say he is? Is that a crime now in Ephesus?'

'There's only one religion here, Mister,' Demetrius growled. 'Diana's. The Jews in the ghetto know that and keep their noses clean. They're as angry with Troax as we are. He's had a go at them already and got very short shrift from the rabbi.'

'In any case,' Suliman said, 'it's not a religious matter. It's a political one. An attack on Diana is an attack on the unions who serve her. An attack on the city which lives under her protection. This isn't just about believing. It's about money. It's time Troax was made to understand that.'

I thought Ferris would certainly agree. 'All right, gentlemen. It's very much a domestic issue as it stands, of course, but I'll see what I can do to give it a wider audience. I'm not interested in rhetoric, nor is my editor in Rome. But if you present it cogently and peacefully I'll do my best to give him a story he'll be prepared to run.'

Which was what they wanted to hear.

After dinner I took a cab across the city and paid off the driver near the ghetto. There was a service going on in the synagogue, the sound of singing filtering into the street. I ordered a glass of wine in a small bar opposite and sat by the window waiting for the congregation to come out, half-hoping Troax would be among them. But he wasn't. Had probably been barred.

When most of the people had dispersed, the rabbi stood talking to a man under the porch light. There was something about him which interested me. He was better dressed than the others and had an air of quiet authority which obviously impressed the rabbi. Eventually they shook hands, the rabbi went back inside

and the man began to walk away. I caught up with him
on the corner.

I introduced myself as a friend of Troax and he was
warily polite to begin with. His name was Gaius, his
home in Philippi. When I said I had visited Troax in the
jail there and had heard him speak in Athens, he relaxed
a little. 'So, you're that Lucas. I've heard him mention
you. A colonel in the medical branch, I believe?'

'Yes. On leave from Troas for a day or two.'

'You were with Paul in Corinth too, weren't you?'

'Briefly. At the home of Aquila Nikolas.'

It was the right answer and he smiled. 'So how can I
help you, Doctor?'

I explained about the planned demonstration by the
unions in the square.

He frowned. 'I was afraid something like this would
happen. Paul's been very outspoken about these souvenir
statues, calling them foolish idols and warning people
not to buy them. There've been one or two unpleasant
incidents in the shops.'

'The important thing now,' I said, 'is to make sure he
doesn't try to disrupt this demonstration tomorrow.
They're intent on getting him arrested and if he's
there...'

'I understand.'

'You'll warn him off, then?'

'I'll try. Aristarchus from Thessalonica is here with me
and he has a persuasive tongue. But you know what
Paul's like. Can't resist a crowd.'

I nodded. 'How is he these days?'

'Back on form. That long rest in Corinth did him a lot
of good.'

'He hasn't mellowed at all?'

Gaius chuckled. 'If anything he's blunter and more reckless than ever.'

Mr heart sank. It was what Suliman was banking on. A public outburst from Troax. Hard evidence that he was an agent provocateur. Evidence the Council could not ignore. 'But you will try to hold him back tomorrow?'

'Of course. For what it's worth.'

But Gaius underestimated his ability to influence Troax. Or perhaps Aristarchus did the trick. Whatever the reason, he wasn't in the square to hear Demetrius' speech the next day.

'Brothers!' Amplified through the loud-speakers, Demetrius' voice rang like a tocsin over the square where the assembled unions packed in under their banners and placards. 'You know our prosperity comes from this.' Standing tall on the temple steps, a row of young priestesses behind him, he held up a silver statue of Diana.

A roar of approval thundered across the square. 'All right,' he said. 'Now you've seen and heard for yourselves what this fellow Troax is doing. He dares to say our goddess is a fraud.'

There were shouts of: 'Blasphemy. Wicked lies.'

'I agree with you, brothers. We know his words are lies. But he has succeeded in convincing many people here in Ephesus, twisting their minds with his slanders. You see the danger here? In ridiculing our craftsmanship he is destroying our livelihood. Oh yes, brothers, he's snatching the bread out of our mouths and the mouths of our children.' He spread his arms wide to quell the furious shouts which greeted these words. 'And that's not all. There's an even greater danger. The danger that this temple to our Lady will be dishonoured and her majesty mocked. The mighty Diana, worshipped by honest people the world over, reviled and rejected because of this mischief-making Jew. A renegade even his own people have turned against. Are we to stand idly by and let this terrible thing happen? Or are we to stand together, brothers in arms, and fight for Diana and for the welfare of our families, the pride of our city?'

Half-a-dozen men, planted in the crowd, shouted, 'Great is Diana of the Ephesians.'

The square erupted as close on five hundred voices took up the chant. 'Great is Diana of the Ephesians.'

Demetrius stood, hands on hips, and let them work themselves up. Then he silenced them with an upraised fist. 'This is not just a matter for the unions. The life of the city itself is at risk here. We shall march through the streets to the theatre and lay it before the people.' He leapt down the steps, seized one of the banners and flourished it high above his head. 'To the theatre.'

The union leaders marshalled their members and led them out of the square, the banners waving like battle-flags above their heads. Ordinary citizens fell in behind them, excited by the noise, sensing trouble. Standing in a shop doorway, I watched them surging past, faces contorted with anger, eyes focused on the banners. Suliman had been right. This was no local disturbance, no peaceful demonstration. This was front-page stuff.

'Ah, there you are, Doctor.' Gaius slipped in beside me, breathing hard.

'Where's Troax?'

'Safe. He wanted to come but we managed to dissuade him – with some difficulty.' He mopped his face, sweat running out of his hair. 'This is beginning to look ugly.'

'And could get worse. Where's this theatre?'

'On the edge of town. An amphitheatre, actually. Used for public spectacles, not all of them very edifying. It's huge. I've seen upwards of two thousand packed in there.'

I thought of what Demetrius could do with that kind of an audience. Not a comforting thought.

'The police have gone to the Town Hall to alert the Council.'

Much good that would do. It would take a military presence to contain a demonstration this big, not a bunch of civil servants. 'Right, Gaius. Let's go and see.'

The amphitheatre was solid with people standing crammed together on the terraces in the glare of the sun. The whole place was seething as more and more came crowding in, confused, excited, aware that something was brewing, not at all sure what.

Down on the stage a man was trying to calm them. A tiny figure far below us, desperately calling through a microphone for quiet.

'Alexander,' Gaius said in my ear. 'One of the leaders of the synagogue and no friend of Paul.'

There was a little lull as he began to speak. 'Citizens of Ephesus.' A strong voice and persuasive. But his Jewish accent was as unmistakable as his black hat and long black coat. Before he could continue the crowd booed him. 'Shut your face, Jew. We haven't come here to listen to your pious mumblings.' And a great shout went up. 'Great is Diana. Diana of the Ephesians.'

Demetrius stepped forward, shouldered Alexander aside and grabbed the microphone. He cupped his ear with his hand. 'What did you say?' He was grinning fiercely, in his element. A maestro in front of a choir of thousands. 'Let me hear it again.'

And the crowd responded with a thunderous, orchestrated roar. 'Great is Diana.'

'And again.'

The people answered him ecstatically; devotees chanting a mindless mantra, deep-throated, united, unstoppable.

Helpless in the press of bodies, I felt my head start to spin. I had seen this sort of thing too many times in my travels; knew it was a build-up to violence and terror. Demetrius had only to make a signal now and they would explode out of the theatre, trampling on each other to get into the streets and run amok, smashing shop-windows, overturning cars, looting and burning and killing in a frenzy of blood-lust.

Suddenly a man appeared on the stage, coming up the steps from the underground dressing-rooms, surrounded by four men in uniform carrying machine pistols. Riot police. Big men and disciplined. They bundled Demetrius aside and stood guard as the man they were escorting seized the microphone. One of them pointed his weapon at the sky and fired a short burst. Magnified by the loudspeakers, the harsh rattle of the gun stunned the crowd into silence.

'It's the Town Clerk,' Gaius murmured. 'In the nick of time.'

I nodded dubiously. Even allowing for the distance between us, he was a small man, dapper in his tailored linen suit, hair neatly combed, face composed. Impressive enough in a court room, skilled no doubt in logic and reasoned argument. But here in this melting-pot of hysterical rage? I doubted even his escort could get him a hearing.

Until he began to speak.

'Fellow Ephesians.' His voice was measured, soothing but with steely confidence. 'Everyone knows that our city is the keeper of the temple of Diana and of the sacred statue which fell from heaven itself. Don't they?'

This was the iron fist of Demetrius in a smooth, velvet glove. The crowd listened tensely. One wrong word and he would lose them.

The Town Clerk smiled, pacing himself skilfully. 'Nobody can deny this. Can they?' He waited a long moment. 'Well then. You must calm down and not do anything reckless. Nobody has desecrated the temple. The goddess is still in her place attended by her priests and priestesses. Is that not so?'

A murmur of assent rippled round the terraces.

'Nor, to my knowledge, has anyone said evil things about her,' the Town Clerk said equably.

This was too much for Demetrius. He broke free from the policeman's grasp and lunged for the microphone, eyes blazing. 'I have proof that she has been...' He gasped with pain, the muzzle of a gun rammed into his kidneys.

'Shut it, my old son. You've had your say.' The policeman put an arm under his chin and hauled him back.

Unruffled, the Town Clerk gave him a little nod. 'If Demetrius and his union members have an accusation to make against anyone, we have the authority and regular days for court cases to be heard. Charges can be tabled. Justice done decently and fairly.'

The people on the terraces shuffled their feet uneasily, muttering to each other, aware that their champion had somehow been cut down to size.

'Of course,' the Town Clerk said in his bland, reasonable voice, 'if there is something more you want?'

A lone voice called, 'We want Troax charged.'

'That is not for the unions to decide, my friend,' the Town Clerk said. 'It will have to be settled in a legal meeting of all citizens, presided over by His Worship the Mayor with the authority vested in him by Rome.'

The same voice shouted, 'We don't need Rome for this.'

'I'm afraid you do. What has happened here today could well result in us all being accused of a riot against the City Fathers, against the law, against Rome itself. There is no excuse for this disgraceful uproar and we would not be able, in the event of it being reported, to give a good reason for it.' He paused, timing it expertly. 'The city is full of tourists, many of whom are men of high repute in their own cities. I want you to think very carefully what kind of a report about us they might carry back home. And how that report would be received.' He smiled. 'Have I made myself clear?'

The crowd's response was a respectful round of applause which began with a few and spread round the whole theatre.

The Town Clerk gave them a little, courteous bow, raised his head and waved. 'Good. Now go peacefully to your homes like the sensible people you are.'

'A tour de force,' I said to Gaius as we made our way out of the theatre. 'He's a remarkable man, your Town Clerk.'

'And could be one of us,' he said ruefully, 'if introduced to the Faith with tact and understanding.'

I smiled wryly. We both knew that was not Troax's way...

'An opportunity wasted,' Troax said with a sigh of regret. 'Had I been in the theatre that day I could've buttonholed the Town Clerk and won him over. And with him the entire Council of Ephesus.'

'Perhaps.' It had always been his dream: to get the support of the civic authorities wherever he went and so legalize the Faith. That was why, in the end he had demanded a trial in front of the Emperor and the Senate. He had tried, and failed, in Athens and pinned his hopes on Rome. Only to be banished to this miserable attic, out of sight, out of mind. 'But not entirely wasted. Your church in Ephesus bears witness to that.'

He smiled. 'A seed sown in secret to blossom openly. I think it's my favourite church. Good people sure of their beliefs.' But insignificant in the life of that city. Without influence, without social standing. 'They send me money, y'know. Generous gifts they can't afford. Embarrassing but well-meant.'

I knew without asking where the money went. Into the church in Rome. For the poor and dispossessed.

'Still,' he said, brightening, 'all things come to him who waits. That's why you're here now, of course. To brief me for my trial.' He shook his head. 'I know you think I was foolish not to accept Agrippa's ruling. But it wasn't the right time or place. I mean, who's ever heard of Caesarea outside Israel? But Rome...' He reached out and touched my hand in a gesture of trust. 'I'm glad you're here to see it, Michael.'

8

'So,' Ferris said. 'I was right. It *is* political.'

That year the winter came unusually early to Rome. October still had two weeks to run and already there was frost on the windows of his office, the banks of the Tiber were fringed with ice. Impervious to cold, he had the heating on but turned down low.

'I'm not sure of that, sir.'

'I am. Your report from Ephesus proves it.' Which was why he had called me back. 'A deliberate attempt to bring the unions into disrepute, bankrupt the city and turn the mob loose on the streets. And it so nearly came off. Would've done but for that Town Clerk. I've put him in for an ORE, incidentally.'

'Well deserved, sir.'

'Yes.' Ferris steepled his fingers thoughtfully. 'A near miss, then. But he's learning fast, our little Roman Jew. Next time he'll bring it off and we'll be in deep trouble.' He got up from behind his desk, walked to the wall map and traced the route with his finger. 'He's got the Aegean staked out all the way round from Ephesus through Philippi to Corinth and back. And his next move's back east to Syria, you say?'

'Since I wrote that report he's changed his mind about that, at least for the moment.'

'Yes? So where is he now?'

'On his way north to Troas. There's a team waiting for him there.' Sopater from Berea, Aristarchus and Gaius, Tychius and Trophimus from Turkey. And Timothy. I reeled off the names.

Ferris's eyebrows rose. 'A General Staff already.'

'If you like, sir.'

'I don't like, Lucas. I don't like it at all. They're just the tip of the iceberg, every one of 'em the leader of a cell.' He shook his head. 'That trip to Syria's just a ploy to fool us. He's coming west to Rome. Has to be. You don't lay a trail from Jerusalem to Corinth, all your bases established and linked, and then turn round and go back. Doesn't make sense. Right?'

I nodded.

'Right, Lucas. Off you go to Troas. High time you had another look at those patients in the hospital there.'

'And this is one of our success stories, Colonel,' Helen, the ward sister, said. 'Flight Lieutenant Eutychus.'

Greg Eutychus. A young fighter pilot shot down over Bulgaria, cruelly abused by his captors, liberated four months previously. The last time I had seen him he had been strapped to his bed in the psychiatric ward, a writhing, sobbing, incoherent wreck totally out of touch with reality. Now he was sitting under the awning outside the Officers Mess tent, composed, at peace with himself.

'I'm glad to see you're living up to your name, Lieutenant,' I said. Eutychus means fortunate; and that, thanks to the expertise of my colleagues, was what he was.

He grinned shyly, his eyes clear and untroubled. 'Thank you, sir.' He glanced at the sister. 'When can I get back to flying?'

'One step at a time, I think.' I saw the sister nod gratefully. 'Where's your home?'

'Derbe, sir. Well, that's the nearest town. My father farms, y'see.'

'Couldn't be better. A spell of convalescent leave in the country. A month or six weeks to get you back on form. Then, if you pass your medical, we'll recommend a stint as an instructor before you rejoin your squadron.'

He frowned. 'I thought I could go back now, sir. Ease myself into things again.'

The sister said quickly, 'He's not ready for that, sir. Not yet.'

'I agree. You've been through the mill, laddie. Made a remarkable recovery. Let's not undo the good work by rushing things, eh?'

'If you say so, sir,' he said, disappointed.

'Good man.' I looked at Helen. 'Is he getting out at all yet?'

'Oh yes. He's been down into the town a couple of times already.'

'Fine.' I grinned at Eutychus. 'Make the most of it. You'll be back in harness soon enough.'

Walking out to my car, Helen said, 'As a matter of fact, sir, I'm taking him out this evening.'

'That's very forward of you, Sister,' I said teasingly.

She blushed; a pretty young woman, neat and slim in her uniform. An evening with her would put a whole new meaning to the phrase 'Tender loving care'. 'It's not like that, sir. Our relationship is strictly professional.'

'I'm sure.'

'It's just that I think he needs to meet people. Not military types, civilians. Come to terms with the real world again.'

I nodded. 'Good therapy.'

'I belong to this group, y'see.'

'Oh? And what group is that?'

'Well, religious, actually. But very informal and easy. I

mean, we don't ram our ideas down people's throats. Just a few friends meeting for a meal and a chat about the things that matter. I think it'd do him good. Give him a new perspective, new hope.'

'Yes, he needs that. Where's your temple?'

She smiled, amused. 'Oh, we don't have a temple. We meet in each other's houses over supper.'

'Sounds very civilized.' I hesitated. 'You wouldn't, by any chance, be Christians, would you?'

'Why, yes.' She gave me a searching look. 'You've heard of us, then?'

I shrugged. 'Snippets of information picked up on my travels.'

'You've heard of Paul Troax, of course?'

'Yes,' I said. 'I've heard of him.'

'He's coming tonight to talk to us.' She smiled. 'He's a remarkable man. Nothing to look at. Quite ugly, in fact. But when he talks – marvellous.'

'So I've heard.' I hesitated. 'You'll not let him put our fighter-boy under any kind of pressure, will you, Sister? He's not ready for that yet.'

'I understand, sir.'

'Only I'm told this Troax is very forthright in his views. A kind of obsession.'

She nodded. 'I hear what you're saying, Colonel. There'll be nothing like that, I promise you.'

'Fine. Take him along by all means. But don't keep him out too late, eh?' I got into my car and wound down the window. 'This house you're going to. It's in Troas, is it?'

She nodded and gave me the address. 'Thinking of coming along yourself, Colonel? You'd be very welcome.'

'Thank you, Helen, but no. I don't want Eutychus to think I'm keeping tabs on him.'

'No, of course not. Some other time, perhaps?'

'Why not?' I said and let in the clutch.

I had intended to get away early but dinner in the mess that evening was a leisurely affair and I was in the best of company, swapping reminiscences with my brother officers, toasting old friends. So it was close to midnight when I parked the car a few yards past the house down the street, got out and walked slowly back.

This was the fashionable quarter set on a low hill above the harbour. A district of tree-lined avenues and imposing, three-storied houses gleaming white-walled in the shadows. A far cry from the ghetto tenements Troax normally frequented. I remembered what Ferris had once said, sitting at his desk with Troax's file open in front of him: 'When he turns respectable and starts targeting he upper classes, that's when we really begin to worry.'

The house I was looking for stood on a corner. In common with its neighbours, the ground floor security shutters were closed for the night. As in Italy, town houses had their bedrooms on this level, the living-room upstairs. There was a telephone kiosk opposite and I crossed over to stand in its shadow. A large window at the top of the house was open to the night air, light pouring out, the muted sound of voices. Or rather of one voice. I smiled to myself, recognizing whose it was. When Paul Troax was in full flow nobody else got a word in edgeways.

Someone was sitting on the windowledge, silhouetted against the light, his back to the street. A square-shouldered man, swaying a little, lulled by the stream of words. I saw his head droop forward and hoped somebody in the room was watching him. It was a long drop to the pavement behind him.

A moment or two later a burst of applause drifted out into the street. The figure in the window started, sat up straight and overbalanced. I was halfway across the street when he hit the ground with a bone-crushing thud. He lay flat on his back, twitched his legs once and was still. I knelt beside him feeling for a pulse. There was none. He stared up at me with sightless eyes, his face set in an expression of surprise. The face of Greg Eutychus. I felt my anger rise. He had come to us a broken man, haunted by terror and pain, lost in a nightmare world. And we had brought him back to sanity, healed his body, restructured his mind. One of our success stories. And now...

I knelt above him, hands locked on his chest, pumping hard to kick-start his heart. The front door of the house swung open and Helen was on her knees opposite me giving him the kiss of life. I went on pumping, aware of people gathering round us. Going through the motions, knowing it was all too late.

Someone said, 'Shall we ring for an ambulance?'

I stood up and said coldly, 'Too late for that. He's dead.' I looked down at the sister's stricken face. 'For God's sake, Helen. You could see he was in a dangerous position up there. Why didn't you do something?' I saw the tears of hurt in her eyes and was ashamed. 'I'm sorry. Not your fault.'

'Let me through.' And that was Troax, elbowing the watchers aside, going down on one knee, lifting Eutychus' head and shoulders, hugging him. 'It's all

right, friends,' he said. 'Don't distress yourselves. He's still
alive.'

Words, I thought angrily. You're good at those, aren't
you? But it's too late. Words can't reach him now.

Troax picked the boy up with surprising ease and
carried him back into the house. 'Just give me a minute,
please,' he said, took him into a downstairs bedroom and
laid him down gently on the covers. He sat beside him,
held his hand and said, 'Now then, Gregory. You've had
your little nap. Time for supper.'

A gasp went up from the people crowding into the
hallway as Eutychus sat up, rubbed his eyes and smiled
apologetically. 'Sorry about that, sir,' he said. 'Bad show. I
must've dropped off.'

Troax grinned at him. 'Oh yes, you did that all right.'
He stood up and helped Eutychus to his feet. 'Come on,
then. Let's go and eat.'

'How did he do that?' Helen said as we followed the
people upstairs. 'There wasn't a spark of life in the boy
and I'm pretty sure his spine was fractured. Skull too,
probably.'

I nodded, remembering that ominous thud on the
pavement. 'I don't know how he did it. It's a gift he has.'

'It's a miracle,' she said, her eyes shining, her face rapt.
'A sign from God.'

'If you like.' We were at the top of the stairs now, the
room in front of us noisy with excited voices. I suddenly
felt uncomfortable. An unbeliever hemmed in by
devotees of a God I didn't know, didn't understand. 'I'm
sorry, Helen. I have to go now,' I said lamely.

'Oh,' she said, disappointed. 'I thought you'd like to
meet Paul. As a doctor, I mean.'

'Another time, perhaps.' I turned and went back down

the stairs and out to my car, my head full of questions. Opening blind eyes, healing a schizoid, putting a cripple back on his feet – yes. I could accept all those things, find a clinical, psychological explanation. But raising the dead? Who could explain that?

I drove down to the harbour and walked along the sea-wall trying to come to terms with what I had seen. Finding it impossible. I wondered what I should put in my report to Ferris and decided to say nothing of what had happened tonight. I had a trustworthy (albeit innocent) informer in the ward sister. I would stay on in Troas and wait for more acceptable news to transmit...

'So it was in Troas, not Ephesus, that I began to get through to you, Michael?' Troax's good eye watched me shrewdly.

It was dark in the room now although the sky was still glowing in the sunset. I stood up and pressed the light switch by the door.

'Not working, I'm afraid,' Troax said apologetically. 'They won't pay for electricity. There's an oil lamp over there somewhere.'

I found the lamp and lit it, setting it on the makeshift bookcase. 'No,' I said then. 'Not Troas, not actually Ephesus. But in the Ephesus church.'

He looked puzzled for a moment and then smiled. 'Ah yes. My farewell speech in Miletus. That got to you, did it?'

'Yes.' I remembered being moved almost to tears in the cargo shed on the Caligula wharf as he spoke to the Ephesian elders who had made the journey to the coast to see him off.

It was a Troax I had not heard before. Not the

impassioned street orator rubbing salt into the wounded pride of the religious authorities; nor the fumbling, would-be scholar in the Areopagus. This was a persuasive speaker, opening his heart to trusted friends, building up their morale, undergirding their faith. Reminding them that he, like them, was empowered by the spirit of the Christ. 'Put yourselves and your families in the Master's hands and you have nothing to fear. Trials and tribulations, yes. Persecution, mockery, hatred, yes. But these are transient things to be borne to the glory of God who calls us to share his suffering as Jesus, his son, shared ours. You have heard the Good News and received it with faith. Teach it to your children, share it with your neighbours, offer it to your enemies. Then my work among you will not have been in vain.' He smiled at them. 'To those who hate us we seem to be of little account; an irritant to be dismissed out of hand. But we are the Christians – Christ's own – and ours is the Kingdom. And in God's good time, we shall prevail.'

Writing my report to Ferris that night, I had been convinced that the heart of the matter was religious; a religion I was suddenly hungry to share. But, of course, those closing words about the Kingdom and its inevitable establishment were the only ones which impressed him, confirming his belief that the whole thing was a cunningly disguised charter for revolution. Like most of us, he only saw what he wanted to see.

'You were spying on me, weren't you?' Troax said now, his voice amused and without rebuke.

'Yes.'

He chuckled. 'So it wasn't just coincidence that we kept meeting?'

'No,' I said. 'I'm sorry.'

'Don't be. It was surely meant that news of my progress should be made known to important men in Rome. That they were made aware of this spread of the Faith. I'm in your debt for that, Michael.'

'And not angry?'

He looked surprised. 'Of course not. And was that why you followed me to Caesarea?'

'Not entirely.' Ferris had lost interest when I told him Troax had gone back to Israel, seeing it as an admission of failure. 'He's bitten off more than he can chew, Lucas. Gone back home to recharge his batteries. So long as he stays there he's no threat to us. But I want to know the minute he comes west again. If he ever does.'

'I followed you there in hope,' I said.

'Of what?'

'Of a faith I could lose myself in. And find myself.'

'Yes,' he said slowly, contentedly. 'I rather thought so. I'm glad you're here, Michael, to see my dream fulfilled. We've shared the journey. It's right that we should share the arrival.'

'I'm glad, too, Paul,' I said, grateful for the shadows which hid the guilt in my face.

9

'In prison?' I said incredulously. 'In Jerusalem?' The cradle of the Christian faith, where he was respected. Not much liked, but respected.

'He's back in Caesarea now, actually.' Over the phone Ferris sounded as puzzled as I was. 'Under house arrest.'

I was in Mersa Matruh at Desert Airforce HQ, conducting a routine inspection of the medical unit there. It was May 54, and the last I'd heard of Troax he had been in Jerusalem consulting with the Church Council there. Or R-and-R, as I'd reported to Ferris. And rest and recreation was what he badly needed – but apparently hadn't got. 'What's the charge this time, sir?'

Ferris grunted. 'Need you ask? He upset the Jews and it all got out of hand. Lysias had to step in a bit smartish to save the feller's life.'

Colonel Miles Lysias, nearing retirement and commanding GHQ in the Antonia barracks. A tough infantryman of the old school, six-foot-two in his socks with the sort of belligerent presence even the Sanhedrin respected.

Ferris chuckled mirthlessly. 'Must've gone against the grain. Lysias has no time for religion. He put Troax in irons and shunted him up to Caesarea with an armed guard p.d.q.'

'So?' I said, knowing what was coming.

'So I want you there by this time tomorrow. Fax me soonest from the Consulate.'

I flew down to Alexandria in an IAF chopper after an early lunch, switched to the Cheops International Airport and got a late cancellation on the El Al flight to Caesarea.

Justin Felix was the consul there, living in some style in Herod's old palace on the hill behind the town. He gave me one of the guest rooms and invited me to dinner. His wife, Drusilla, was an excellent hostess with a lively mind and a good sense of humour. Good-looking too, in a dark-eyed, Jewish way. Which was just as well, for Felix himself was poor company; a lanky, awkward man with a large bony head made all the more gaunt by his cropped black hair. I don't remember him smiling once during the meal. Whenever I glanced at him he was staring at me with uneasy eyes, picking at his food, confining himself to ungracious, meaningless comments. How she had fallen for him I couldn't imagine.

Afterwards, when Drusilla had tactfully left us to our brandy, he said abruptly, 'You're here about Troax, aren't you, Lucas?'

I saw the suspicion in his face and admitted I was interested in the little Jew.

'Why?' he said bluntly.

I shrugged. 'Professional interest. I'm interested in a mind balanced on a fine edge between intellectual brilliance and hallucinosis.'

He made an impatient gesture. 'Your medical jargon means nothing to me. But I know a fanatic when I see one. The man's deranged. Any fool can see that. Nobody in his right mind puts himself at risk for the sake of a dead religious maniac. It's a fantasy, Lucas, and a dangerous fantasy at that.' He shook his head gloomily.

'He may be an interesting case to you but from where I sit he's a threat to the authority I exercise in this province in the name of the Emperor.'

'You've talked to him, I take it?'

'I've questioned him, yes. Asked him what the hell he was playing at inciting law-abiding citizens to riot.' The gaunt head loomed at me across the table, red spots of anger in the sunken cheeks. 'Said it was a treasonable offence.'

'And?'

'He denied it. Said the whole thing was an unfortunate misunderstanding.'

I hid a smile, imagining Troax's quick mind adroitly turning Felix's clumsy questions against him. 'He's probably right. This is, after all, one of the provinces where religion's taken seriously and...'

'Seething with unrest under the surface.'

'Perhaps. But if that's true...'

'Of course it's bloody true. What's needed here is a firm hand.'

What's really needed, I thought, is justice tempered with understanding. The minimum use of force if and when persuasion fails. 'Is that why you've got him locked up?'

'House arrest. It's more comfortable than he deserves.'

'Pending trial, presumably?'

He shook his head. 'I've done that. Had the High Priest up here with a lawyer. Chap called Tertullus. Good man. Knows his stuff. Told me Troax had been stirring up trouble from here to Greece. Tried to do the same in Jerusalem and came unstuck. Tertullus said they'd had the matter in hand and we were all set to give him a fair trial according to their religious laws. But that

old warhorse, Lysias, put his oar in and sent him up here
for me to deal with.'

'Ah,' I said. 'So that's how it was?' Lysias passing the
buck with his usual hard hand.

'It could all have been settled here if he'd had the
sense to keep his big mouth shut,' Felix said bitterly. 'But,
of course, he demanded the right to speak and
harangued us with the same old story about Jesus
Davidson being raised from the dead.'

'Which didn't go down well with the High Priest?'

'Damned right it didn't. Put me in a very awkward
position. I mean, I need his support and confidence if
I'm going to keep things ticking over comfortably here.
I don't like him much – very self-important and a prig
with it – but I need him. So I adjourned the court,
promising to look further into the matter, and remanded
him in custody. Let him stew for a week or two, hoping
he'd come to his senses.' He pursed his lips disgustedly.
'But when I talked to him again we were back on the
old merry-go-round of goodness and self-control and all
that pious claptrap.'

'What will you do now?'

'Nothing. I've clipped his wings and tucked him away
where he can do no harm.' Felix grinned unpleasantly,
big teeth between thin lips. 'A few months of that and
my guess is he'll either come to heel or go off his head
completely.'

'I wouldn't bank on that,' I said, concealing my dislike
of the man. Properly administered, Roman law was a
model of its kind. But in the hands of ignorant men like
Felix it was a travesty of justice. 'You've had him checked
out medically, have you?'

His eyebrows rose. 'What for?'

I shrugged. 'Well, its s.o.p. isn't it? While he's in your custody he's your responsibility, Felix. He's done a lot of travelling, most of it dog-rough. Could be harbouring all kinds of bugs. Malaria, hepatitis, typhoid, even. If he dies on you it could be embarrassing.'

He frowned, a little frightened. 'Well, I... he looks fit enough to me. Physically, anyway. Mentally he's obviously unstable.'

I smiled. 'Appearances can be deceptive. Would you like me to have a look at him while I'm here? Just to be on the safe side?'

'If you like,' he said grudgingly. 'You might even talk sense into him. In the presence of one of my staff, of course.'

'Naturally.' That was Felix's way. Everything by the book...

'It wasn't too bad,' Troax said, his face worn and tired in the lamplight. 'Not at first, anyway.'

Until Felix, grown tired of waiting for him to co-operate, had moved him out of house arrest and thrown him into one of the cells beneath the palace, manacled like a dangerous criminal.

I said, 'That business in Jerusalem. What was it really all about?' It was not something we had been able to discuss when I had visited him with one of Felix's secretarial staff taking notes. I had checked his blood pressure, sounded his chest and cleared up his bad eye. He had been underweight and the arthritis had begun to claw his fingers. Otherwise there had been nothing a good rest, good food and freedom from stress could not have fixed.

He sighed now, remembering. 'I handled it clumsily,

I'm afraid. I wasn't expecting trouble, y'see. Not there in Jerusalem. James Davidson was the leader and doing a good job, as you'd expect from one of the Master's brothers. More than a thousand Jewish Christians in the city itself and steadily growing. They welcomed me with open arms. Made a real fuss of me. Invited me to address the Council...'

Which was when it had all gone wrong. Nobody had warned him that they were Jews first and Christians second. Worshipping in the Temple, keeping the Jewish feasts, the Jewish rituals. For them the Christian faith was no more than an extension of the faith of their fathers.

'They had a built-in distrust of anyone who was not a Jew, Michael. And that meant the majority of people in the churches I had founded outside Israel. They insisted that all Christians, of whatever nationality, should observe the Jewish rites of worship and diet and dress, be faithful to the ancient law of Moses. And, of course, I couldn't accept that.'

Some of the Jews had accused him of taking Gentiles into the temple. There had been angry scenes and the makings of a full-scale riot. Only Lysias's intervention had defused the situation by removing him to Caesarea for his own safety.

'If you hadn't dug your heels in and insisted on being tried in Rome,' I said, 'you might still be a free man.'

Troax gave me a rueful smile. 'That's what Agrippa said.'

'He did his best to help you, y'know.'

'Yes. He's a just man. Not like those wolves in Jerusalem. They'd have run me out of the city and stoned me if Miriam hadn't intervened.'

'Your sister?'

He nodded. 'She sent her son to Lysias and he reacted very quickly indeed. Did you ever meet her, Michael? I can't remember.'

'Just once. A long time ago...'

Back in the 40s, in fact, when I was still piecing together details of Troax's early background, looking for clues to his personality. The sort of man he had been until he changed sides.

I happened to be near Tarsus and decided to take a couple of days off and have a look at the place. Originally a small town in south Turkey, it had become famous for its university and, in particular, its school of Stoic philosophy housed in a complex of pseudo-Greek buildings well away from the industrial area. I put up in a decent hotel near the campus in an avenue of expensive shops and students' bars, changed out of uniform and went in search of the ghetto. It was there I found the Troax factory built round three sides of a cobbled yard, screened from the street by a high wall.

Presuming me to be a customer, the porter directed me to the office across the yard.

The girl behind the counter in the reception area was well-spoken with dark, lustrous eyes and a briskly courteous manner which matched her neatly tailored clothes. I didn't need to read the name-plate on the counter to know she was a Troax. Two or three years younger than Paul but the family likeness was there. Glossy black hair, firm chin, slim build. She asked me politely if I had an appointment.

I said I hadn't but would like to see the owner.

'And you are, sir?' she said.

'Michael Lucas.' I saw the name meant nothing to her.

'I'm sorry. My father's not here. He's gone to see a supplier and won't be back till tomorrow. Is there any way in which I can help you?'

'It's not a business visit, Miss Troax. I happen to be a friend of your brother and...'

Her eyebrows rose. 'Saul's sent you?' She seemed surprised and a little nervous.

'Not exactly.'

And now she was wary. 'You're not from the police, are you?'

I smiled, recognizing the ghetto reaction to a well-dressed Roman arriving out of the blue. Her eyes went to the window as if expecting a police car waiting outside the gates. 'I'm a doctor, actually.'

'Oh.' She stiffened in her chair. 'Saul's not ill, is he? I mean, it's not bad news of him?'

'When last I saw him he was extremely fit. Rarin' to go, you might say.'

She smiled, relieved. 'Yes, he's like that. Always in a hurry. Look, please sit down. It's good of you to come. Would you like some coffee?' She went to the percolator bubbling on a small table. 'Black or white?'

'Black, please. No sugar.'

She brought the cups and sat down opposite me. 'I worry about him. He pushes himself too hard sometimes. Overdoes it.'

I said carefully, 'As he did in Damascus?'

Her eyes flickered. 'You know about that?'

I nodded, hearing again that irascible voice in the darkened room on Straight Street. The frustration bordering on panic.

'Is it true he went blind there?'

'A temporary blindness. Psychological. He had a

disturbing experience and his mind refused to respond to his eyes for a while. It's not an uncommon reaction to shock. And there's no lasting damage.'

'So he said in a letter.' She shook her head, her black hair swinging. Attractive in a Jewish sort of way. 'I don't understand these things, I'm afraid. But whatever happened there changed him completely. Now he's become a stranger to us. My father won't have his name spoken in the house, refuses to acknowledge his existence. We're orthodox Jews, Doctor, and it's all been too much for us.'

'I understand.'

'Do you?' She looked at me, half-puzzled, half-accusing. 'He was always so obedient. Revered our laws and customs like a true Pharisee. My father was so proud of him. And now...' She sighed, leaving the sentence unfinished.

'I think you ought to know that he's still very much a Jew at heart,' I said gently. 'He goes to the synagogue on the Sabbath. Still holds fast to Moses and the prophets.'

'And looks for the coming of Messiah?' she said levelly.

'Ah.' I sipped my coffee, aware that we were on dangerous ground. 'He believes that Messiah has come.'

'Davidson the carpenter.' She almost spat the name at me and I knew it was her father talking. All the disappointment, all the righteous anger. 'And he still calls himself a Jew?' There was bitterness there. And shame.

'A Christian Jew yes,' I said, wishing Paul were there to speak for himself, wash away her doubts in a torrent of words. 'I appreciate your difficulty in accepting that, Miss Troax, but what he's trying to do is reconcile his

Jewish religion with the Faith which Davidson taught and which, as Paul sees it, is a universal religion open to men and women of all races and creeds. I'm afraid it's made him a lot of enemies.'

'That's what worries me, sir. He's a very sensitive person, easily hurt.'

This was news to me and must have shown in my face for she smiled. 'I know. He hides it behind a forceful, almost brash, manner people find disturbing.'

I nodded, remembering that dinner party in Cyprus; the shouting match between Paul and Elymas. 'That's certainly true.'

'But underneath he's very vulnerable. Aware of the effect he has on people. Unable to control his feelings.'

I saw the cup shaking in her hand as she struggled to defend him. 'I'm sure you're right, Miss Troax,' I said lamely.

'When we were growing up together he was marvellous to me. Gentle, sympathetic, quick to comfort.' She sighed, her eyes bright with memories.

'My father is a good man and I know he loves us but it doesn't always show.' She made a face; amusement tinged with apology. 'Like so many highly moral men he's intolerant and tends to be very angry over what are really trivial misdemeanours. And Saul shielded me from his displeasure, taking the blame that was really mine. And the consequences which were not always pleasant. It's not something you forget.'

'No. I can understand how...'

The phone rang and she excused herself and picked it up. 'Troax of Tarsus. How can I help you?'

I stood up and went to look out of the window. Across the yard in the loading bay men were stacking packs of canvas tents on a truck. I watched them without really seeing them, my mind busy with what she had told me.

I was beginning to understand the complexities of Paul Troax. Under the surface of his dynamic drive, his impatient, bull-at-a-gate dogmatism was a kind of childlike innocence which could fill him with compassionate joy and also, if he was thwarted, with a bitter anguish of the spirit.

There was Saul the Jew, doomed by his race to be an underdog; a second-class citizen scorned alike by philosophical Greek and pragmatic Roman. A scapegoat, with all his kind, for the ills of society, to be bullied and spat upon and cursed. Taking the blame, as Miriam had said, and the consequences.

And there was also, in the same scrawny body, behind the same ill-favoured face, Paul the Christian Roman; a free-born spirit, servant to no man but Davidson from whom he drew his strength, in whose persona he delighted, to whose cause he had dedicated his life.

This was a formidable dichotomy which would have destroyed a lesser man. An internal war fought daily in his mind between good and evil, hope and despair, life and a living death. How long could a man – any man – survive such a conflict?

She put the phone down and I resumed my seat.

'Sorry about that,' she said, smiling.

I grinned. 'Business is business.' I drank the last of my coffee. 'So you don't see much of him these days?'

Her smile died. 'We don't see him at all, Doctor. My father has forbidden him to come home even for one night. He writes to me occasionally. Fortunately I deal with all the incoming mail in the office and can hide his letters from my father who would burn them unopened.

I share them with my mother. She's heartbroken, poor dear, and finds them comforting although she weeps over them. We both know we'll never see him again.'

I thought it ironic that a religion which had created a nation out of a rabble of fugitive slaves could be so divisive, setting fathers against sons, making enemies of friends. 'I'm very sorry, Miss Troax. It must be hard for you.'

'And for Saul.' He would always be Saul to her. Saul the brother, not Paul the apostate. 'We are taught to honour our parents, y'know. And he's always done that. To have honour rejected must be agony for him.'

'Yes.' An agony all the more terrible for being suppressed, every jaunty step he took trampling on his deepest emotions, his most treasured memories. Yet out of the pain, the sense of guilt for antagonizing his father, for those years of hounding the original followers of Davidson – out of this had blossomed a religious movement which thrived on adversity and which, under his leadership was beginning to spread westward across the Empire. A religion without priests, without a Temple, which the Jews called blasphemous and Ferris called treason.

'This Davidson cult,' she said. 'It's political, isn't it? Jews and Gentiles united against Rome. Plotting against the Emperor.'

'I honestly don't know but I think it unlikely. Davidson himself was religious, not political.'

'They say he was a king, though.'

I shrugged. 'They have many names for him.'

'Saul thinks he was Messiah.' She looked at me steadily. 'Do you?'

I smiled. 'I'm a Roman, Miss Troax, not a Jew. And we

Romans manage well enough without religion. I expect you find that hard to understand?'

'I do, yes. Religion – the true religion – is our life. As it was once Saul's.'

'And still is, believe me. Only now he has not just inherited his Faith, he has discovered it for himself.'

'There's a difference?' she said, puzzled.

'If you could see him now,' I said gently, 'you wouldn't ask that question.' I stood up. 'I've taken up too much of your time, I'm afraid. Thank you for your hospitality. And for being so frank with me. I've learned a lot about your brother this morning. As a doctor specializing in psychology I find him fascinating. If it's any consolation to you, I think he will make a name for himself of which you would be proud.' I held out my hand and she took it with a shy, uncertain smile close to tears.

'It's been a relief to be able to talk about him,' she said. 'I only hope I haven't said too much.'

I smiled back. 'What you have told me I shall treat as a confidence. In my profession that's sacred.'

'Thank you, Doctor Lucas,' she said. 'You're very kind.'

And then the tears came...

'She's one on her own, my sister,' Troax said, his good eye lighting up with pride. 'Her father's daughter in many ways.'

Her father, I noted, not his. He had found a new father in God, healing old wounds, tempering justice with mercy. Every speech I had heard him make over the years confirmed that. Listening to him you forgot the ranting voice, the ugly face; heard only the astonishing power, saw only the transcendent beauty of the spirit in the man. 'Is she still in Jerusalem?'

'Yes. We still write to each other.'

So that bond, at least, had held firm. 'She's no longer running the office, then?'

'No. When her father died she sold the business and used some of the money to fulfil a long-held ambition. To make the pilgrimage to Jerusalem at Passover. It was there she met her husband. He's a tailor with a shop in Hillel Street in the city centre. It was love at first sight and they've made a good life for themselves there.' It was said wistfully; the wistfulness of a gypsy for a settled life beyond his reach. 'Tobias is their only child. Came late in the marriage and is a source of great pleasure to them both. Good-looking boy and clever with it. When he left university he joined the Civil Service and has done well. Quite high up the ladder now, I'm told.'

'Ah,' I said. So that was how he had been able to persuade Lysias to step in and rescue his Uncle Paul from the hard-liners in the Sanhedrin. The old alliance between the civil and military authorities. A favour for favours received.

If only Felix had been so decisive...

'That fool Felix,' Ferris growled. 'How he ever made consul I'll never know. Greased a few palms and licked a boot or two probably.'

Sitting opposite him across his desk, I said, 'He wouldn't be the first.' The Diplomatic Corps was riddled with nepotism and bribery. 'Done us a service, though, sir. Taken Troax out of circulation. No more riots, no new churches.'

But he wasn't listening. 'All we needed was another Ephesus and we'd have nailed him. Executed for treason. File closed.'

It was two years since Troax had been arrested in Jerusalem. Two years in which Felix had done nothing except hold him without a trial. I said, 'It's as good as closed, anyway.' I had spent the time doing my official job; visiting hospitals in every command in the eastern Mediterranean, working with patients, persuading the Treasury to pump more money into the facilities. 'I've covered the ground he pioneered and there's been no sign of any organized defiance of the law. Without Troax to spur 'em on they're beginning to wither.' A machine without an engine, without fuel.

'You think so?' He tapped a file on his desk. 'This tells a different story, Lucas. We've been intercepting his mail and it makes uneasy reading. All wrapped up in religious mumbo-jumbo, of course. Pastoral letters to his churches, he calls them. But if you read between the lines the message is plain enough. Corinth, Philippi, Thessalonica, Ephesus – even Rome, damn it. All urged to keep the Faith and prepare themselves for the Day of Judgment.' He smiled grimly. 'That's his code word for revolution. Well, it's coming for him sooner than he thinks. Felix is retiring this month – not before time in my opinion – and there'll be a new consul in Caesarea. Porcius Festus.'

'Ah,' I said.

'Ah, indeed. On the ball, our Festus. Ambitious, clever, impatient of red tape.' Ferris rubbed his hands together like a hungry man called to the table. 'We'll see some action now he's in the saddle. Not a man to drag his feet. He'll hand Troax over to the Jews. It's what they've been clamouring for and he needs to keep them happy. Then there's Agrippa, newly appointed to the provincial throne. Festus has got to work with him, win his confidence, establish a rapport with him.'

I nodded. Another puppet king for Rome to manipulate.

Ferris pushed the file aside dismissively. 'Troax is for the high jump. No doubt of that. The Sanhedrin's never forgiven him for changing sides and he'll get short shrift from them once they get their hands on him. And with him out of the way, forgotten in an unmarked grave, we can put the frighteners on those so-called churches of his. Pick out a couple of local leaders and make an example of them. Shut down the whole treacherous network once and for all.'

I pointed out that the Sanhedrin had no power to execute prisoners. Especially Roman prisoners.

'No problem. Lysias's boys'll do the necessary, backed by Festus.'

I nodded unhappily. It was Jesus Davidson and Pontius Pilate all over again.

'One last trip for the Firm, then,' Ferris said briskly. 'Marcia's got your flight booked. Festus'll put you up in the consulate. Make sure it's all tied up and no loose ends, eh? A satisfying conclusion to the work you've done for us. Then you can go back to being a full-time shrink again. Yes?'

I murmured something about retiring from the army, living quietly somewhere up north. And was mildly surprised to find I meant it.

He tilted his head, smiling. 'You'll not find me ungrateful, Mike. I'll see you're handsomely rewarded. Oh yes. A colonel's pension from the Medical Corps plus a lump sum bonus from the Firm. That should set you up nicely.'

It was, I thought, an unfortunate turn of phrase.

10

'I heard you might drop in, Colonel,' Festus said, not sure of me, feeling his way. Which meant he'd had a signal from Ferris.

I murmured something vague about being in the area and bringing him greetings from the Senate, congratulating him on his appointment. He tapped his nose conspiratorially; a neatly chiselled nose, as Roman as his cool grey eyes, his patrician haircut. A handsome, smiling man who knew precisely what he wanted and how to get it. 'Nuff said, old boy. Glad to have you aboard my little ship of state. More a mine-sweeper than a battlewagon, I fear, but trim enough and not without potential.'

He had only been in residence about ten days but had already stamped his personality on the place. His office on the first floor of the palace was newly furnished, expensively and with taste. It was difficult to imagine how untidy and run-down it had been under Felix. Now leather-bound books filled one wall from floor to ceiling. I suspected they had been bought by the yard and never opened but the effect was impressive. As were the silver-framed photographs on his desk, the marble statuette in one corner which looked like a genuine Praxiteles – and probably was – and the high-tech computer at his elbow. He had brought his personal staff with him from Rome; hand-picked young men exuding polite efficiency. And a squad of muscular types in dark suits to take care of security.

'You'll be here for the big day, of course?' he said, probing.

'The big day?'

'Absolutely. Day after tomorrow, HM King Agrippa and his sister, the Lady Bernice, will be here. A state occasion when Rome and Israel meet as friends and colleagues to put this province back on the map.'

'I see.'

'Of course you do, old boy.' He smiled complacently. 'All a bit low-key after Rome, I grant you. But we do our best. Show the flag with pride, eh?'

'I'm sure.'

He leaned forward over his desk. 'Actually, I've got a surprise for our new monarch. A legal matter about which I shall ask his opinion. A formality, really. I've already got it all buttoned up. But it pays to let our little puppets think they're pulling the strings occasionally.'

'I'm told HM's an intelligent man with a good grasp of the law.'

He nodded. 'So I believe. Especially Jewish law. I'm banking on that. It's an interesting case. A Jew who is also a Roman citizen. Which makes it a bit tricky, as you'll appreciate. Way beyond my predecessor's ability to handle. His reaction was to do nothing. Something he was rather good at. Troax has been held in prison here for almost two years.' He shook his head. 'Pathetic and quite unnecessary.'

'Troax?' I said, feigning surprise. 'Paul Troax?'

'You know him, do you?'

'I know of him. Isn't he the leader of this Christian sect?'

'He likes to think so. The Jewish Christians in Jerusalem don't agree.' He shrugged dismissively. 'It's religious, obviously. Anywhere else it wouldn't matter. But religion is big in Israel and Troax is a cancer that needs decisive surgery, if you'll forgive the medical metaphor.'

'I'm a psychologist, not a surgeon.'

'Quite so. Anyway, my instinct was to get it sorted quickly and be done with it. I'm not a man to tolerate others' mistakes. I went for the leaders of the Sanhedrin and had Troax up in front of them to explain himself. Which he did at some length. Tedious stuff well above my head. But they reacted fiercely, demanding I let them take him back to Jerusalem for trial. Which, of course, is what I wanted them to say. Get him off my patch, y'see? But...'

'But?'

'But he played his trump card. Said he was a free-born Roman and, as such, appealed to Caesar for trial in Rome.'

I hid a smile, imagining the effect this must have had. 'That *is* his right, of course.'

'Absolutely. "You've appealed to Caesar," I said, "and to Caesar you will go."'

'When?' I said.

'Good question, old boy. The thing is, I don't want to begin my stint here – which, by the way, I'm reliably informed could lead to better things – Yes, well, I don't want to get off on the wrong foot by sending an insignificant little man to Rome for trial, do I? I'm here to see justice done on my own patch, not go running to the Senate with every little problem. That's why I want to bring Agrippa in. If he can persuade Troax to be tried by Jewish law, I'm off the hook. Troax goes down to Jerusalem in chains. The Sanhedrin condemns him as a subversive and demands an execution. The army takes the strain and we all come up smelling of roses. Agrippa because he starts his reign with a decisive action. I because I've saved the Senate from the bother of dealing with the fellow. Neat, eh?' He smiled, pleased with himself. 'I'm damned glad you're here, Lucas. Your professional opinion might be useful. From what I've seen of Troax he's not altogether with it. Got the twitch, as you military people call it. Mentally unstable. Your field, I believe?'

I nodded.

'Splendid, my dear fellow. Absolutely spot on. You'll not object, then, if I call you as an expert witness?'

'My pleasure,' I said, clutching at straws. Given the opportunity to address the court, Troax would condemn himself out of his own mouth. If I could get in first...

In the event I wasn't given the chance.

The court was convened with much ceremony in the great Audience Hall of the palace before a large company of VIP's. Military brass-hats in full fig, members of the Caesarea City Council in ermine-trimmed robes of office, Sanhedrin rabbis black-cassocked, black-hatted, Jewish Christian leaders from the capital rather over-shadowed in their best suits – a formidable array to deal with so small a prisoner.

We all rose as Agrippa and his sister made their entrance and took the places of honour on the rostrum. The usual speech of welcome and appreciation was made by Festus wearing the uniform of an honorary colonel of the Praetorian Guard, savouring the occasion, doing it in style. Agrippa listened attentively. He was younger than I had expected – in his middle 30s – with an aristocratic face and all the built-in dignity of his status. A small smile played about his lips but his eyes were everywhere, identifying, assessing. I decided if anyone could keep Festus in his place, he could.

When the consul had finished, with commendable brevity, Agrippa responded cordially; a carefully prepared reply which stamped his authority on the assembly with tact but also with force. I looked at him with sudden hope. This was no ordinary puppet king. This was a man who knew his own mind.

Then Troax was brought in, flanked by two armed guards who towered over him. I was dismayed to see the manacles on his wrists and ankles. An unnecessary precaution designed to humiliate him, presenting him to us as a dangerous criminal of unsound mind. His face had filled out a little since I had last seen him but he was woefully thin, weighed down by his heavy chains. He took his place in the dock meekly enough and was greeted by fierce hissing from the rabbis. I saw his head come up, his good eye bright with anger, his clawed hands gripping the rail in front of him like talons. Cage an eagle for two years and the shine goes off his plumage. But he's still an eagle.

The clerk of the court called for silence and Festus rose again, now in the role of prosecutor. 'Your Majesty, Lady Bernice and all who are gathered here today.' His voice rang round the great hall, every head turning towards him. This was where the power lay. Agrippa was king but Festus was the Emperor's consul. 'This is Paul Troax, the man against whom all the Jewish people, both here and in Jerusalem, have brought complaints to me. They demand that he should no longer be allowed to live.'

The rabbis nodded approvingly, exchanging hard smiles. But their pleasure was short-lived.

Festus shook his head slowly. 'I have to tell the court that I have not found him to be guilty of any offence meriting the death sentence.'

The Jews stared at him in disbelief. Agrippa's eyebrows rose. Bernice stifled a yawn behind a polite hand. Festus waited, timing it carefully. 'Furthermore, Your Majesty, I must also tell you that he has made an appeal to Caesar.' He shrugged. 'He is fully entitled so to do, of course, since he is a free-born Roman.'

The city councillors looked at each other in surprise.
'Is this true?' Agrippa said.

'Quite true, sir. And it puts me in a quandary for I have nothing specific to write to the Emperor about him. Rumours, yes. Religious speculations – I might almost say fantasies. But nothing His Imperial Majesty would take notice of.' Festus spread his hands. 'He would not thank me – nor you, sir – for wasting his time with such matters.'

This brought the rabbis to their feet, shaking their fists, protesting vehemently. The clerk of the court had to shout to silence them.

'That is why I have brought him before this court,' Festus said. 'And in particular before you, Your Majesty. So that, after you have examined the case against him, I may have something cogent to write. For it seems to me unreasonable to send a prisoner to Rome without clearly indicating detailed charges against him.'

Agrippa nodded gravely. 'I agree. Accusations of guilt must be firmly established and presented if we are not to appear foolish to the Senate. That much is obvious, surely.'

Sitting beside Festus I felt my heart sink. It had all been arranged between them, king and consul conspiring together to set a trap for Troax. One he would be unable to resist walking into. And so it proved.

Agrippa looked directly at Troax. 'You have permission to speak on your own behalf, Paul Troax.'

Troax straightened his back. His chains rattled as he stretched out his right hand in the orator's attention-demanding gesture. 'Your Majesty, I consider myself fortunate that I am to defend myself before you against all the things the Jews accuse me of, particularly since you are so well acquainted with our Jewish customs and religious rites. I ask you then to hear me with patience.'

It was a good beginning, reminiscent of his speech to the Areopagus. But it was followed by a sustained attack on the Jews. Turning in the dock to face them, he said, 'Why do you find it impossible to believe that God raises the dead?' It was a gauntlet flung disdainfully in their faces. The old fire was back in his voice and burning brightly. Perhaps his defeat in Athens still rankled. Perhaps this was his revenge for that humiliation. Whatever the reason, he had the bit between his teeth and was unstoppable.

He took us back to the beginning – his zealous persecution of the original followers of Jesus Davidson; his extraordinary experience on the Damascus road; his commission to go to the Gentiles in Turkey and Greece, offering hope and forgiveness and the power of the Spirit. Telling it well, with passion and a kind of transparent honesty which held the attention of us all. 'And so, Your Majesty,' he said, winding up to his climax, 'for the last twenty-four years until my imprisonment without a trial here in Caesarea, I have travelled widely, establishing Christian churches in many towns and cities, welcoming Turks and Greeks and Romans into the Kingdom. This is why the Jews – my own people – seized me when I was in the Temple in Jerusalem and tried to kill me. But always, through much suffering and injustice, I have been helped by God. And now I stand here in his name to share with you all, king and consul and commoners, Jew and Gentile alike, the glory of his Son, Jesus the Christ.'

The uproar in the hall was as furious as it was sudden. It took the clerk almost five minutes to restore order.

'Why are you all so angry – and so blind?' Troax said then. 'What I say is exactly what Moses and the prophets foretold, as you well know. That the Messiah, whom the Greeks call the Christ, must suffer and be put to death. And be the first one to rise from the dead and proclaim the truth of the Kingdom – which is in this world but not of it – to all, whatever their race or language. In this truth I stand this day before you, a man of no account in your eyes but filled with the spirit which cannot be quenched. You may destroy me but the truth you cannot silence. For I know beyond all argument or denial that he who rose from the dead and returned to his friends in the Spirit will hold me in his hands through suffering and imprisonment – yes and through death itself if needs be – and bring me safely home to him.'

This was too much for Festus, aware that his hold on the assembly was being challenged. He stood up and shouted at Troax. 'You're mad. That's patently obvious. Your great learning has addled your brain with absurd fantasies. No man in right mind would believe such rubbish.' He swung round to face Agrippa. 'Your Majesty, I have an expert witness I would like to call at this point. A specialist in the disorders of the mind. He will tell you that...'

Troax cut in coolly. 'Oh come, Your Excellency. Mad? You know that's not true. Your expert witness has seen the things I am able to do by the power of God, setting people free from the horrors that haunt their minds and cripple their bodies. Making them whole again and free. Can a madman cure the insane? Ask Colonel Lucas.'

Festus hesitated, opened his mouth, closed it again and sat down.

'No?' Troax said. 'Not going to risk it?' He smiled. 'Well then, what I have said here today is the sober truth. The only truth. The truth of the grace of God made known in Jesus the Christ. Pontius Pilate didn't understand it. Nor do you. But that is not important.' He bowed to Agrippa as to an equal. 'Your Majesty, you know I'm right. Porcius Festus has tried to discredit me by calling me mad. Is this the only charge he can bring against me?' He smiled. 'Let me ask you a question, sir. Do you believe in the prophets? The prophets and him who came to fulfil their words in his life and death and resurrection? I know in my heart you do.' And now his voice was composed, his face radiant; as if, behind the king he could see another, greater King. 'Of course you do.'

Watching him I knew what he expected, what he had spoken and sweated for. A word of assent from Agrippa. Two minds meeting in total accord, meshing together in a mutual acceptance of the Faith. So the answer, when it came, was like a glove flicked contemptuously across his face.

Agrippa chuckled, amused. 'In this short time, Paul Troax, do you really think you can make me a Christian? My life changed instantly by what you have said? An interesting speech, if a little fanciful. But a life-changing speech?' He shook his head pityingly. 'Now that *would* be a kind of madness,' he said and was rewarded by a relieved sigh from the assembly as the tension Troax had screwed up to breaking point finally snapped.

I saw Troax's shoulders sag, a look of bitter disappointment on his face as he realized that in Caesarea, as in Athens, he had failed.

For God's sake, man, I thought, haven't you got it into your head yet that you're not in the same league as kings and scholars? You're a man of the people – the poor, the insignificant. You speak their language, share their hopes, tell 'em what they've always wanted to hear. That's where you power lies; in your little churches seeded across the Empire, keeping the faith while the world passes by uncaring. Among them you're a giant. Here you're a pigmy.

But a gallant, dogged pigmy. His head came up again, undefeated. 'Whether a short time or a long one,' he said with a kind of compassion, 'I pray to God that you, sir, and all this assembly who have listened to me today might become what I am.' He lifted his manacled hands and added wryly, 'Except, of course, for these chains.'

Agrippa shook his head smiling. There was admiration in that smile and something else. A wistfulness. A touch of regret.

Festus nodded to the clerk who said, 'Take him down.'

Festus made a diplomatic little speech thanking us all for our patience. Agrippa smiled graciously, took his sister's hand and came down on to the floor of the hall. We were all on our feet by then and as he passed by, the king paused in front of Festus. 'A strange man,' he said quietly, 'but, I think, an innocent one. He could have been released today had he not appealed to Caesar. See he is properly cared for and make all speed to send him on his way to Rome.'

Festus hesitated. 'The Sanhedrin will not thank you, sir, for rescuing him from their clutches.'

'Nor would the Emperor,' Agrippa said, 'for delivering a Roman into their hands.'

'I have a favour to ask of you, Lucas,' Festus said that evening when we were sitting on the balcony after dinner enjoying the cool sea air. 'I want you to go with him. Take him to Rome for me.'

'Why me?'

'Because I'm still convinced he's off his head and shall write as much in my report.'

'Yes?' I said warily.

'Well, I've got to write something, damn it. Something Nero will understand.'

'A dangerous fanatic creating havoc wherever he goes?'

'Exactly. And if I send him in the care of a psychiatric expert of your rank and standing it will add weight to the idea.'

I nodded. 'I suppose so,' I said, knowing Ferris would approve.

'So you'll do it?'

'Providing he goes unmanacled and by sea.' Unmanacled because I would not subject Troax to the humiliation of chains. By sea because I knew he would be imprisoned as soon as we arrived in the capital to await Nero's pleasure and I wanted him to have his last journey in comfort with a chance to recoup his strength. 'As my patient, not my prisoner.'

Festus looked doubtful. 'There'll have to be an armed guard y'know, old boy. For appearances' sake.'

'I understand that. But I want it done discreetly and with the minimum of stress. After all, he's not likely to jump overboard. He may be subject to curious moods and fancies but he's not suicidal.'

'I have your professional word on that?'

'Yes.'

Festus stood up and went to the balcony rail, staring out over the sea; a hard man under the urbane surface, but not a vindictive one. He turned round. 'So be it. There's a cargo ship with passenger accommodation loading for Ostia. I'll arrange a booking for you both. You don't mind sharing a cabin with him?' He smiled thinly. 'I'll get him cleaned up and fitted out with some decent clothes. Make him respectable.'

'Fine.'

'And you'll take full responsibility for him?'

'Of course.'

'That's settled then.' He made a wry face. 'I don't envy you, old boy. A religious maniac's likely to be poor company on a longish sea voyage. He'll probably talk your head off every mile of the way.' He grinned. 'Might even persuade you to become a Christian.'

I looked at him sharply and he flushed apologetically. 'Just joking, Lucas. No offence meant.'

'Or taken,' I said.

11

'What's the charge?' Ferris said. 'Treason, I hope?'

I was phoning him on a secure line from the Consulate, a copy of the indictment Festus had prepared in front of me. 'Nothing so definite, I'm afraid, sir.' It was, in fact, a masterpiece of diplomatic gobbledegook liberally laced with legal jargon, specifying little more than an accusation of making a public disturbance.

I gave Ferris the gist of it and he snorted. 'Typical. Festus is too damned clever by half. Always has been. Look after number one and to hell with the truth. Doesn't matter. We can get our legal boys on to it here and let them sort it out. Fortunately our beloved Emperor's intellectual ability is limited. He'll accept whatever we choose to tell him.'

'Perhaps,' I said dubiously. 'But what I've got here's a non-starter. A junior just out of law school could rip it to shreds in five minutes.'

He chuckled. 'Just so long as you've got something with an official stamp on it. That's all we require. That, backed by the evidence you've collected over the years, will cook his goose. The main thing is he's walking straight into the trap.'

But it wasn't like that. I'd had a talk with Troax, told him what we were planning to do, and he'd been jubilant. 'It's exactly what I want, Michael. Two years of waiting and hoping come to fruition. I don't mind telling you I was worried. Afraid I'd be dealt with here. Quietly put down and no questions asked. All my work discredited by a handful of minor officials. But now.' His face had lit up. 'Rome, Michael. The seat of power. Where I've always wanted to be.'

'You could've gone yourself from Ephesus or Corinth as a free citizen.'

'And been arrested the minute I stepped ashore. Clapped into some small-town jail without a trial and left to rot.' He shook his head. 'This way I go straight to the capital to be tried before the Emperor in the Senate. That's front-page stuff and I intend to make the most of it.'

Ferris said in my ear, 'And you're bringing him by sea?'

'Aboard the *City of Patros*, yes.'

'May one ask why?'

'If we want to present him to the court as a dangerous traitor with an international organization behind him he'll need to be in good shape physically. At the moment he's well below par. Just a harmless crank with a bee in his bonnet. No threat to anyone. A sea-voyage will buck him up. Show him to be the reckless firebrand we know him to be. Properly handled by a good prosecuting team he'll really put on a show.' Every word I was saying was tongue-in-cheek. But a trial before Nero was what Troax wanted. The grand climax he'd set his heart on. I reckoned he deserved his moment of glory.

'Point taken,' Ferris said. 'The *Patros*, you say? That's a freighter.'

'Yes.'

'Calling at several ports en route?'

'I believe so. Is that a problem?'

He grunted. 'You'll have to keep a close watch on him, Lucas, or he'll be off at the first opportunity and disappear into the woodwork again.'

I smiled. That was the last thing he'd do. 'I'll make sure he arrives on schedule, sir.'

'You do that. We don't want any last-minute hitches on this one.'

Aboard the SS City of Patros

8.9.56 *Two days out of Sidon where we called in to take on more cargo, mainly grain. This is one of the City Line's oldest ships, travel-stained, slow and ponderous in the water. Her old-fashioned superstructure — single tall funnel, masts fore and aft, two massive derricks over the cargo hatches — gives her a top-heavy appearance which promises heavy rolling in all but the calmest of seas. Fortunately the weather is good so far.*

The passenger accommodation is surprisingly comfortable, the cabins large and airy, the dining-saloon well-appointed in a dated, brass-and-mahogany way. We take our meals there with Captain Ximos, the deck officers and Vigor, the chief engineer, together with half-a-dozen merchants and their wives, served by uniformed stewards.

Spartus, the guard commander, also eats with us and has a cabin opposite ours. He's a veteran infantry major going home on retirement; heavily built, balding, with a florid complexion. Amiable enough in a gruff, stolid way, he's obviously been briefed by Festus to carry out his duties unobtrusively. There's always a guard at the end of the passageway between the cabins, two more stationed on the boat-deck where we take our daily exercise before relaxing in canvas chairs. But it's all very low-key and casual. At least on the surface.

Festus was as good as his word and Troax looks quite

*respectable in a charcoal-grey suit, not new but pressed
and cleaned, with a white shirt and black shoes. Nothing
can disguise his shortness of stature, the suppurating eye,
the clawed fingers. He'll always be an ugly little man; a
caricature in an anti-Semitic cartoon. It's only when he's
in full cry on a street corner that the hidden strength and
passion come through. Then he's magnificent.*

So far, so good, then. But there's a long way to go.

17.9.56 *Myras, Turkey. Off-loading a consignment of
timber from Lebanon. The weather continues fair and
warm and Troax's health is steadily improving. He's
eating well and more at ease than I've ever seen him.
Sometimes in our cabin before we go to sleep he
reminisces about his adventures. He has an astonishingly
accurate memory and it's fascinating to hear the events
I've witnessed described from his point of view. But at
meal-times he's largely silent, albeit in a companionable
way. I suspect he is already beginning to rehearse his
defence — and relishing it.*

*The other passengers treat us with a kind of wary
respect. Festus, with his usual attention to detail, briefed
Ximos to fend off any awkward questions about us with
vague hints that we are boffins working on a top-secret
project concerned with chemical warfare for the Ministry
of Defence. This neatly explains our reticence in
company, my medical insignia and the presence of our
bodyguard.*

*Troax was indignant when I told him. 'I'm not
travelling under false pretences, Michael.'*

*'You're travelling as my prisoner,' I said. 'And I make
the rules. So guard your tongue in public. All right?'*

He grinned. 'No politics in the mess, is it, Colonel?'

'And no religion either. Especially no religion.'
'As if I would,' he said.

20.9.56 *Terapetra, Crete. A busy day for the deck-*
hands as two pieces of heavy agricultural machinery — a
tractor and a combine harvester — were winched aboard
and shackled to the main deck between the hatches. They
make the ship look even more unstable; dangerously so,
in my opinion. Troax says they know what they're doing
but I'm not so sure. A feeling shared by Vigor. I saw
him this evening morosely kicking the chains which
secure them; a lean, wiry figure in oil-stained overalls.
He's a Phoenician, with the narrow face and slightly
pointed ears of his race, and has all the engineer's
mistrust of the deck crew.

'Worried, Chief?' I said, smiling.

He gave me a sharp look. 'Angry, sir. We're way
overweight already. Puts my engines under a strain, see?
I know it's the cargo that makes the profit for the
owners. But these two monstrosities — ' he kicked the
chains disgustedly — 'bloody stupid.'

'She's a big ship,' I said.

'And an old one,' he said darkly.

When I told Troax he shrugged. 'Marine engineers are
notoriously pessimistic, Michael. The captain knows
what he's doing. Don't worry about it.' He grinned. 'I'm
not.'

'You never worry about anything,' I said.

He looked surprised. 'What's the point? We're in
God's hands.'

22.9.56 *Lasea, Crete. We limped in here this afternoon*
for repairs. Vigor was right to be concerned. Twelve hours

*out of Terapetra a bearing in the prop shaft began to
overheat and we had to reduce speed.*

*Relations between Vigor and Ximos are distinctly
fragile. Ximos is a large man, red of face, hair and beard
with a temper to match. He has a bluff, avuncular
manner with the passengers; the archetypal sea-dog with
a fund of salty, improbable stories (of which he is always
the hero) to tell over dinner. But his eyes betray a deep-
rooted uncertainty I find disturbing. Half an hour in his
company and you realize why he commands the ageing
ugly duckling of the Line and will never be promoted to
a flagship. And resents it. Most of the time he and Vigor
rub along together well enough but in any kind of a
crisis they are quickly at loggerheads. It doesn't make for
a happy ship.*

25.9.56 *We are back at sea en route for Syracuse with
the new bearing fitted. Ximos is all smiles again, eager
to make up lost time. But Vigor is still moody.
Apparently, when they stripped the shaft down,
considerable wear was discovered. He is not happy about
this, nor about the high revolutions Ximos is demanding.
The Patros is a single-screw vessel with nothing in
reserve if the shaft fails. Ximos has half-promised him a
new shaft when we get to Syracuse where there are
excellent facilities for repairs. But this is the long leg of
the voyage and if things go critical in the engine-room
we could be in real trouble.*

*Fortunately the weather is holding. Calm sea, blue
sky, warm sun. Long may it continue.*

*Troax is making plans to contact the little Christian
church in Syracuse as soon as we dock and ask them to
get word to Rome that he is coming. He's full of bounce*

*and looking forward to seeing Peter Johnson again.
Johnson's now the Christian leader in the capital and
Troax is talking of an affectionate reunion with him.
'We haven't always seen eye to eye, y'know,' he said to
me this morning as we strode round the boat-deck after
breakfast, 'but under that rough exterior he's pure gold.
In everything that matters we're of one mind.'*

*I haven't the heart to tell him he'll be going straight
into prison and is unlikely to be allowed visitors.*

28.9.56 *I'm writing this in our cabin and with some
difficulty. Just before sunset today a force ten gale came
out of the north-west and hit us like a giant sledge-
hammer. Black clouds, riven by lightning, spilled out
torrential rain. Roped together for safety, the deck-hands
worked frantically, driving extra wedges into the hatch
covers, reinforcing the chains securing the combine and
the tractor, the thunder cracking like gunfire over their
heads. Now we're butting into the rising sea, rolling and
pitching wildly, the screw racing as the bows dive steeply
into the troughs and the stern lifts high out of the water;
a cockleshell boat in a maelstrom.*

*There were only six of us in the dining-saloon
tonight. Most of the passengers are down with sea-
sickness and Vigor ate in the engine-room, refusing to
leave his beloved machinery. Ximos put on his nothing-
to-worry-about act, assuring us that such storms are to
be expected at this time of the year in these waters and
tend to be ferocious but short-lived. He promised it
would blow itself out by morning. A brave effort but not
very convincing.*

*Troax is sitting up in his bunk reading, quite
unperturbed. To him the storm is simply a manifestation*

*of the power of God; awesome but not to be feared. I
envy his composure but cannot share it.*

30.9.56 *Forty-eight hours into the storm and no sign
of it abating. If anything, it's gaining in strength.*

*Between decks all is chaos. The dining-saloon is a
shambles of splintered furniture and broken crockery,
water swirling ankle-deep over the ruined carpet. There
have been a number of minor casualties – cuts and
bruises and a steward with a fractured arm – and we are
confined to our cabins. More seriously, the top section of
the foremast has been carried away taking the radio
antenna with it and we are unable to send or receive
signals. Visibility from the bridge is down to a hundred
yards; and we blunder blindly on hoping no other vessels
are in our vicinity. The ship creaks and vibrates
alarmingly as if about to break up around us.*

*But Troax is still certain all will be well and says,
with a kind of arrogance, that God has not called him to
Rome only to lose him on the way. He's beginning to
irritate me.*

1.10.56 *We were wakened from fitful sleep in the early
hours of this morning by a rumbling sound which
vibrated ominously through the ship, shaking us as we
lay strapped in our bunks. It was followed by a screech of
tortured metal and a series of heavy thuds. The ship
listed sharply to port and seemed likely to turn turtle.
She hung like that for two long minutes and then
slowly, grudgingly began to right herself.*

*'You know what that was, Michael?' Troax said. 'The
combine's broken loose and gone overboard. The best thing
that could happen. She'll ride more easily now, you'll see.'*

169

And so it has proved. The wind has dropped a little, though still dangerously strong, and we are ploughing on sluggishly, battered but still afloat.

2.10.56 *The worst of the storm is over and we are able to leave our cabins at last. The sea is still very rough and the wind fierce but it has stopped raining and the sky is clearing slowly. For what that's worth.*

This morning there was an air of relief about the ship as we ventured on deck along the lee side, cold and hungry. The galley has been out of action for the last three days. No hot food, no coffee. We've been living on sandwiches and beer. But we had begun to hope again. Until this afternoon.

Spartus suggested we went up to the bridge and had a word with Ximos; what he inevitably called a sit-rep. We found the captain perched on his high chair peering through the salt-encrusted glass screen, his face haggard and hollow-eyed. We've seen nothing of the sun since the storm began and he's been navigating by dead reckoning, unable to get a fix. When Spartus tactlessly asked him what our position was he shook his head impatiently. 'Your guess is as good as mine, Major, but I fear we've drifted too far south to make Syracuse.'

'The Libyan coast, then, is it?' Spartus said gloomily.

'Not if I can help it,' Ximos said.

I shared his anxiety. That barren desert coastline has been the graveyard of many fine ships lured ashore by false lights lit by Arab pirates, to be pillaged and torched, their cargoes rifled, their crews murdered.

I looked down at the main deck; the timber scarred and splintered by the lost machinery, the broken shackles flailing the hatch covers, the sea surging up over the port side where the railings had been ripped out. They seemed mortal wounds to me but when I said so Ximos shook his head. 'Superficial damage, Colonel. Looks worse than it is. The hull's still sound.'

'And low in the water,' Spartus said.

'No problem,' Ximos said. 'The wind's easing steadily now. Give it another hour and we'll start jettisoning the grain. Give us a bit more buoyancy.'

Spartus grunted. 'The owners won't like that. No machinery, no grain. An expensive voyage, Captain.'

Ximos shrugged. 'The insurance'll take care of that. My first priority is the ship. They'll not thank me for losing her.' He looked up at the sky. 'All we need now is a sight of the sun to give us a bearing.' He smiled his wise old sea-dog smile. 'Cheer up, gentlemen. We're not finished yet. Bloody but unbowed, eh? Something to tell your...' He broke off in mid-sentence as a tremendous thump shook the deck under our feet. Through the voice-pipe we could hear a great hiss of steam, a confusion of startled shouts from the stokers below. The throb of the engines died away, the heart of the vessel stilled. 'What the hell's going on down there?'

The ship's head began to drift away, the great wheel slack in the helmsman's hands.

'No steerage way, sir,' one of the sailors called hoarsely.

Ximos growled acknowledgment, working the brass handle of the telegraph angrily as if trying to re-start the engines. A useless gesture.

The door at the back of the bridge slammed open, letting in a gust of wind and spray. We swung round to see Vigor standing there, smothered in oil and beside himself with rage, his eyes blazing in the pallor of his face. 'Damn you, Ximos. Satisfied now are you, you old fool?' he said bitterly.

'Why have you shut down the engines?' Ximos rapped. 'I'm in command here and I make the decisions.'

'The bloody shaft's sheared, that's why. My engine-room's wrecked. Oil temperatures off the clock. Men scalded. Water coming in through the shaft tunnel and a couple of sprung plates. The pumps going flat out and hardly coping. It's the end of the road for you. You're finished. We're all finished.'

Bad news travels fast through a stricken ship and while he was still speaking, members of the crew appeared on the boat-deck and began to pull the covers off one of the lifeboats and swing out the davits.

'Stop those men,' Ximos shouted. 'We'll need every hand we've got if we're to get out of this alive.'

Spartus slid down the ladder and moments later his soldiers were dragging the men back, chopping through the falls with axes and dropping the boat overboard. The sea picked it up and smashed it to pieces against the ship's side.

Ximos clicked on the loud hailer. 'Don't just stand there, damn you.' His voice boomed above the turmoil of wind and sea. 'Get those hatch covers off and start dumping the grain sacks. Handsomely now.'

I thought it a futile gesture but it gave the men something positive to do and eased the tension slightly.

So now we're drifting through the darkness, dead in the water, a battered hulk at the mercy of the wind. A company of frightened people, cold, hungry, without hope. Even Troax is a little subdued, though still insisting all will be well.

❖ ❖ ❖

3.10.56 *Another day and miraculously we are still alive.*

We spent the night on the bridge with Spartus, huddled down round the unmanned wheel, guarded by the soldiers against an increasingly mutinous crew; Ximos dozing on his high chair, Spartus very much in command. I must say the old warrior has come up trumps in this crisis, his authority growing as Ximos becomes more and more withdrawn.

At dawn the sun at last broke through the thinning clouds and we got wearily to our feet to stare ahead through the screen. The wind was noticeably lighter, the sea heavy but smoother, huge rollers lifting and carrying the ship.

We heard it before we saw it; the thunder of breakers on the shore. We looked at each other despondently.

Spartus gripped Ximos' shoulder and shook him awake. 'Libya?'

By now we could just make out the white line of surf and the dim shapes of low hills rising behind.

Ximos stiffened, reached for his binoculars, focused them and grinned tightly. 'Not Libya, Major, thank God. I know that skyline well. It's the north coast of Malta.'

Troax gave me a triumphant look. 'It's going to be all right, Michael.'

'We're not ashore yet,' I said doubtfully. And, to Ximos, 'What're our chances, Captain?'

He looked at me, hollow-eyed, his bearded face crusted with salt. But when he spoke the old confidence was back in his voice. He was in command again; the only one who could get us through. 'If the wind holds steady I'd say the odds are in our favour, Colonel.'

'In the boats on an open beach through that surf?'
Spartus said incredulously. 'Talk sense, man.'

Ximos met his stare with a reproving smile. 'There's a
good harbour further west, Major. With any luck we'll
fetch up there. Or near enough to be towed in by tugs.'
He pointed forward. 'See, the current's turning her
westward and the wind's veering west.'

Spartus shook his head. 'I hope you're right, sir. For
all our sakes.'

Two hours later we were close inshore and no sign of
any harbour. Slowly, inexorably, the ship was settling
under us. The main deck was awash by now, the hull
rolling heavily in the shallower water. The thunder of the
surf which had given us hope now sounded like a death
knell. Ximos, refusing to accept defeat, ordered the boats
to be swung out. The waves seemed to leap up as if to
snatch them away.

Ximos said with a kind of manic calm, 'I suggest,
Colonel Lucas, you and Mr Troax start assembling the
passengers on the boat-deck. And you, sir,' he turned to
Spartus, 'will kindly assist them with your soldiers.
Nothing like a military presence to quell panic.'

'The feller's off his head,' Spartus growled as we went
down the ladder from the bridge. 'No boat can live five
minutes in this sea. We know it and so does he.'

'What's the alternative?' Troax said. 'Stay on board
and watch her break up under our feet?' He shook his
head. 'That's no answer, Major.'

So we went to our boat stations with our fellow
passengers, some grim-faced and stoic, some weeping
hysterically. We huddled on the tilting deck, buffeted by
the wind, the angry sea waiting. It was like being in
bedlam; the hiss of the sea racing past only feet below,

the howl of the wind, the booming of the breakers, the
pitiful cries of the passengers. The ship lunged and I took
a step backward to keep my balance. Something hard
pressed into my kidneys. I turned my head and saw two
of the soldiers behind us, one of them with his machine
pistol rammed in my back.

'What's this?' I said angrily.

The soldier jabbed me again, his eyes cold. 'End of
the line for you, chum. And your little side-kick.
Whoever you are, you're our responsibility, see? We're
not carrying the can if you get ashore and fall into
unfriendly hands waiting to squeeze your secrets out of
you. We'd be for the chop if you did.'

'And if you kill us?'

He shrugged. 'Dead men tell no tales.' He cocked the
pistol. 'No hard feelings, eh?'

Suddenly Spartus was there, knocking the gun aside
with a sweep of his arm. 'What in hell d'you think
you're doing, man?' he barked.

The soldier faced up to him. 'Just doing my duty, sir.'

'Over my dead body.'

'Suit yourself, Major, sir,' the soldier said and turned
the pistol on him.

As the muzzle came up, the ship dug its stem into a
sandbank. The stern rose like a lift, sending us all
tumbling along the deck. There was a harsh grating
sound as the hull twisted and began to buckle, the deck
splitting open, planks ripped apart like paper. The whole
stern section collapsed and fell away, opening the vessel
to a great inrush of water. Through the loud hailer on
the tilting bridge Ximos was shouting, 'Abandon ship.
Jump for your lives. Abandon ship. Abandon ship.'

On the main deck one of the derricks tottered and

*crashed down, taking the foremast with it. The ship was
in pieces. There wasn't a moment to lose.*

*I grabbed Troax's arm and pulled him to his feet.
'Can you swim?' I yelled above the tumult of the raging
sea and rending steel plates.*

He shook his head.

*'Stay with me.' I gripped his arm tightly and pulled
him over the rail and into the sea.*

*We dropped into the crest of a wave, went under and
were immediately seized by the current. We surfaced,
gasping for breath, the water icy cold. Our life-jackets
kept us afloat, carrying us away from the stricken vessel
towards the shore. All around us heads were bobbing,
people shouting to each other. The sea was filthy with oil
spilling out of the ruptured fuel tanks and strewn with
wreckage. A splintered deck plank rammed into us and I
got an arm over it, heaved Troax across it and hung on.
Without it I doubt we would've lasted to the beach. I
suppose we were no more than a couple of hundred
yards from the shore but it seemed like a mile before we
came hurtling in through the surf and felt the shifting
shingle under our feet.*

*I half-carried, half-dragged Troax clear of the water
and staggered back to help other survivors, wading out
chest-deep with Spartus and some of his men. Tough
little Vigor came in minutes later with Ximos close
behind him. They were the last two. Incredibly, the whole
company — passengers, soldiers and crew — came safely
ashore, half-drowned, cut and bleeding, coughing up oil
and water, but alive.*

*'What did you expect?' Troax said when I told him.
'God wants me in Rome. He won't sacrifice others to
get me there.' He grinned, cheerful as ever in spite of*

everything — an irrepressible gnome, his hair plastered to
his skull, his face streaked with oil. 'Let's hope he finds
us a better ship for the last leg, eh?' He turned and
looked inland at the green fields behind the beach. 'So,
this is Malta. I hope we'll be here long enough for me to
do some useful work.'

'Forget it,' I said, shivering in my sodden clothes. 'If
you blow our cover you'll never get to Rome.'

'Um. I suppose you're right. Pity, though. I'd've liked
to add one more church to my list.' He looked at me,
concerned. 'You're shivering.'

'We all are.' Delayed shock, sodden clothes, the wind
cutting. 'Except you.'

He grinned. 'I don't feel the cold.'

You wouldn't, I thought, with that fire in your belly.
And marvelled at the inner strength of the little man,
his incredible ability to bounce back, battered but
astonishingly alive.

'We had a good time in Malta,' Troax said, 'in every
sense of the word. Have you still got that personal log of
the voyage?'

I nodded. Wrapped in a piece of oilskin it had
survived the wreck and was in the safe in my study at
Tremezzo with my private papers. 'Among my
souvenirs, Paul.'

He tapped his head. 'Mine are all in here. Safest place.'

'You haven't kept a written record, then?'

He looked surprised. 'No. Why should I? If I'm to be
remembered it will be for my churches, not for me. All
I've ever done is pass on the message. That's what counts.
Not the messenger.'

I smiled. 'As you did in Malta.'

He shrugged. 'Opportunity only knocks once. Every day a new beginning, every night a consummation. Life's too short to worry about tomorrow. Or yesterday.'

12

'... listed among the ships missing, feared sunk,' Ferris said, a distant voice over the short-wave transceiver. 'We've been passing the hat round for your memorial stone, Mike.'

'Touching but premature, sir. I'm fine.'

'And staying with Mercer, you say?'

'Yes.'

It was ten o'clock in the evening, eight hours since we had been rescued off the beach by Mercer's estate manager who had organized a convoy of ex-army three-tonners to ferry the passengers and crew to Valetta, arranged for the soldiers to be billeted in a barn on the home farm and driven Spartus, Ximos, Troax and me to the villa in his Fiat Torino station-wagon. Leo Mercer was the proconsul in Malta. In his late forties, tall, well-groomed, courteous, with steady grey eyes in an honest face, he epitomized the kind of governor who made Rome great: all the breeding, all the authority, but expressed with understanding and a kind of grace. He had gone out of his way to make us welcome, providing hot baths, comfortable rooms and a change of clothing whilst our own clothes had been dried and pressed (even the buttons on my uniform polished).

'Troax is all right, is he?'

'Very much so.'

'Your cover's not been blown, I hope?'

'No.' Spartus had put Mercer in the picture and the consul had accepted it.

There had been one potentially difficult incident.

Over tea in the villa's spacious lounge, Mercer had apologized for not coming himself to the beach. 'You'll think me very ill-mannered, gentlemen,' he said. 'But my father is seriously ill and could not be left.'

'That's Brigadier Philip Mercer?' Spartus said. 'A fine officer.'

Mercer nodded. 'It's a poor way to end a distinguished career, I'm afraid.'

Troax dabbed at his bad eye, suddenly alert. 'What's the matter with him?' he said with his usual bluntness.

'Dysentery and a high fever,' Mercer said. 'He's too old to cope with that. My doctor had arranged to get him into the intensive care unit in the Valetta hospital but the storm put paid to that. Now he's too ill to be moved.'

'May I see him, please?' Troax said more gently.

Mercer looked doubtfully at the little man in a suit too big for him. 'Are you a doctor, sir?'

'No. But Colonel Lucas is.'

'I see.' Mercer gave me a frank look, as one officer to another. 'In that case, Colonel, I'd value your opinion. I'll take you up to his room.'

Troax shook his head. 'Just tell us where he is.'

Going upstairs, I said, 'This could put me in a very awkward position, Paul. He needs a physician, not a psychologist.'

'He needs me, Michael. I can cure him.'

I thought of the cripple in Lystra, the fortune-teller in Philippi, the young fighter pilot in Troas. Especially him. But it was all a long time ago when Troax had been free and at the height of his powers. How much of that had atrophied in two years in prison?

The old man lay in a darkened room, flushed with fever, dehydrated, desperately thin and wasted. He was muttering incoherently in delirium, his eyes fixed and staring. I felt the weak, thready pulse under my fingers, the erratic beat of his heart and shook my head. 'We're too late. He'll not last another day.'

But Troax wasn't listening. He sat on the bed and laid his hand on the patient's bony chest, his head bowed, his lips moving soundlessly. There was a moment or two of absolute stillness in the room, broken only by the old man's laboured breathing. Then Troax said firmly, 'Be well, Philip Mercer. God has healed you.'

Perhaps it was imagination brought on by tiredness and the reaction to the day's events, but I felt a presence in the room, as if an electric current were sparking and crackling around us. I clenched my fists against the force of it, watching the dying man, my heart racing, my mind numbed. Then it happened. His breathing changed, deep now and strong; easy and without strain. His eyes focused on Troax.

Troax smiled; a tired smile but triumphant. 'Welcome back to health, my friend. And give God the glory.'

I wouldn't have believed it had I not seen it. Philip Mercer sat up. His hollow cheeks filled out, healthily pink, his eyes bright and clear. 'Are you a friend of my son, sir?' His voice was crisp like the voice of a young man.

Troax nodded. 'How d'you feel now?'

'Hungry.' He looked down at his arms, skinny and blue-veined. 'Look at me. I'm like a ghost.'

And you very nearly were one, I thought.

Troax grinned. 'Ghosts don't get hungry. A few good meals and you'll be fine.' He stood up, small and stiff and weary. But oddly commanding. 'We'll leave you to get dressed now. See you downstairs at supper, eh?'

'Yes, indeed. And thank'ee. I don't know who you are but you've saved my life.'

As we walked to the door, I said quietly, 'How did you do that?'

'You know how, Michael.'

Outside on the landing, Leo Mercer was waiting for us. 'How is he?' he said anxiously.

'Just himself.' Troax smiled. 'He's very hungry. When did he last eat anything?'

'Five — no, six days ago. But surely...'

'No wonder he's a bit peckish. He's coming down to supper when he's dressed.'

Mercer looked at me, wide-eyed, puzzled. 'You mean you've cured him, Colonel?'

'God has cured him,' Troax said simply.

'Leo Mercer's very good value,' Ferris said now. 'Whatever you do, don't let Troax upset him with all that left-wing, pseudo-religious claptrap.'

I smiled, wondering how he would react if I told him what had happened. 'Of course not. Actually, they're getting on rather well together.'

'I'm sure,' he said sardonically.

'So what's the next move, sir?' I said, changing the subject. 'Another ship?'

'Eventually, yes. They're a bit thin on the ground at the moment. Those still afloat are queuing up at the dockyards for repairs. You could be stuck there for quite a while. I'll see what I can do to get you a priority booking but it'll take some time.'

In the event we were on the island just over a month before boarding a tanker out of Alexandria bound for Italy, diverted to Malta by Ferris to pick us up...

'Now that *was* a ship, Michael,' Troax said now.

I grinned. After the old *City of Patros*, the *Leviathan* had lived up to her name; huge, stable and surprisingly fast. Her captain, briefed to ask no questions, gave us the full VIP treatment and we lived like lords. So we sailed majestically to Syracuse and on up the Tyrrhenian to Ostia and Rome. 'Happy days,' I said, remembering.

'Yes. I can still see it as though it were yesterday.'

I heard the wistfulness in his voice (a rare indulgence) and grieved for him. He had travelled hopefully, full of confidence, his speech to the Senate completed and rehearsed.

But the arrival had been a dismal anticlimax.

I heard someone coming up the stairs outside, the stamp of the guard's feet as he saluted, and looked at my watch.

'Time you were off, Michael?'

''Fraid so.'

'Dinner in the mess, is it?'

I nodded. From a truckle bed in a garret to the splendour of silver on the long, polished table. From reminiscences of hardship and suffering to the civilized urbanity of conversation over the port. From the menace of the streets to the security of the military brotherhood. It had always been like this. Our friendship limited by the army, my loyalties divided. 'I'll be back in the morning, Paul, to get you out of here. Comfortable quarters, decent food, a change of clothes.'

'Thank you, old friend. I'd like to be presentable before the court.' He smiled wryly, his raddled face pale in the lamplight. 'It's more than they allowed my Master.

They dragged him in front of Pilate in his working clothes, tired and hungry and abused by the soldiers.' He tilted his head with a kind of pride. 'But he still looked like a king. Still dominated his captors and his judges. They were all frightened of him, y'know. The Sanhedrin, Caiaphas, Pilate. All afraid of the country boy with the power of God in him.'

As you were of Stephen Michaelides, I thought but was careful not to say. He had paid dearly for his part in that savage murder. And found forgiveness in his own suffering.

There was a knock on the door and Raynaud came in – a brisk, smart alien from another world. The real world of power politics and unforgiving laws. 'When you're ready, sir,' he said, saluting.

I stood up and made a point of shaking Troax's hand in front of Reynaud. 'Until tomorrow, then,' I said and went out into the night like Judas.

PART TWO

1

'Telephone for you, Colonel.'

It was gone eleven and I was sitting in the mess bar enjoying a final whisky with a medical colleague before turning in. 'Who is it?'

'Brigadier Ferris, sir,' the sergeant steward said, stiffly correct in his white tunic, his face impassive.

I excused myself and went to the phone booth. 'Lucas here, sir.'

'My office. Now,' Ferris rasped.

I had left him there half an hour earlier after a last run-through of tomorrow's operation. Everything checked and double-checked, all the pieces slotted together, looking for flaws, finding none. He had wished me good night cordially. But he wasn't cordial now.

When I got there, Reynaud was with him, looking worried. Ferris nodded me to a chair. 'How was Troax when you left him, Mike?' he said.

'Fine. A bit keyed-up. Excited, as you'd expect. But just himself. Why?'

'Not suspicious?'

'No. He's convinced he'll be addressing Nero and the Senate before this week is out. Looking forward to it. Relishing the prospect. Grateful for the opportunity at last.'

'You're quite sure of that?'

'Absolutely. He – he trusts me completely.'

Ferris and Reynaud exchanged glances.

'Is there a problem?' I said.

'Perhaps. You'd better tell him, Piers.'

Reynaud said, 'Troax had a visitor after you left him

this evening, Colonel. It was noted in the guard commander's daily report.'

'One of the women bringing him something extra for his supper?'

'A man, actually. Jewish. Gave his name as Bargenus. The guard frisked him for a weapon, found none and let him in, leaving the door half-open as per instructions. He was there for the better part of an hour, talking.'

'About what?'

Reynaud shrugged. 'We don't know. They spoke in Aramaic. According to our records he's never been before.'

'Nor have we any knowledge of a man of that name,' Ferris said.

'Wait a minute,' I said. 'Bargenus, you say?'

Reynaud consulted the report. 'Bargenus, yes.'

'Or Bar Jonas. It's a common enough Jewish name and there are many Jewish Christians in Rome. Could be any one of them.'

Ferris looked at me steadily. 'If you know who he is you'd better tell us, Lucas.' His use of my surname was a subtle hint. We were no longer talking as friends but as spy-master and agent.

I hesitated. 'What was he like? Have we a description of him?'

'The guard says he was a big, hulking man,' Reynaud said. 'Six foot two and broad with it. Bit of a bruiser. Broken nose, shock of white hair, big-fisted. Macho as all get-out.'

'Ah.' It was probably just a coincidence but the timing was unsettling. A man of Johnson's stature and personality would be taking an enormous risk bluffing his way past the guard and on this night of all nights. It seemed unlikely but the city was full of spies and informers thriving on rumours. Had he come because I'd been recognized by someone when I went into the house? Paul's friendly medic and confidant turning up out of the blue to visit him after all these years? And had Troax told him why I'd come?

'Well?' Ferris said impatiently.

'I don't know for certain but it could be Peter Johnson. He fits the description.' And would relish the danger.

Ferris nodded gloomily. 'My feelings exactly. There's something afoot here I don't like the sound of. Two Christian leaders putting their heads together. A last-minute rescue we can't afford. Nero would be only too delighted to have two men to throw to the lions. And all our careful planning goes down the pan.'

I shook my head. 'Troax won't wear that. He wants this trial. Set his heart on it.'

'And bring Nero down on the Christians?'

'Only if the verdict goes against him. He is confident it won't. He almost got to Agrippa, remember?'

'Well he won't get near Nero,' Ferris said. 'My guess is this Johnson character went there tonight to dissuade him. God only knows what they're cooking up between 'em.' He turned to Reynaud. 'The guards are expecting you at 07.00 hours?'

'As we arranged, sir, yes. We're due in Romulus by 07.50.' Romulus was the IAF Station down the Appian Way, whence we would fly Troax on the first leg of his journey.

'So we go earlier. 05.00 hours.'

Reynaud looked doubtful. The whole complex operation, involving the army and the airforce at this end, a naval corvette at the other, was timed to the minute. 'It's a bit late to do that, sir. Everybody's briefed right down the line. If we change the schedules now we could come unstuck. Too many people asking too many questions. Security out of the window.'

I knew what he meant. Troax would be travelling as one of Ferris' agents to take control of a special mission in the Aegean islands. None of the Services liked doing CI2's dirty work and would see any last minute changes as dangerous incompetence.

'I agree,' Ferris said. 'We don't want him hanging about on the airfield. But you could be driving into an ambush in that back street, Piers.'

'We can cope with that, sir.'

'I don't doubt it. But it'd take time and throw the schedule out. Not to mention the inevitable publicity when the media find out.' He shook his head firmly,. his mind made up. 'No. We go in early and hide him away somewhere until he's due in Romulus.' He gave me his fierce grin. 'Which is where you come in, Mike. We're collecting him in an ambulance, right?'

I nodded.

'So we hide him among the ambulances at the Stella.' The big military hospital south of the city. 'There's always a fleet of 'em in the ambulance park there. Give you the chance to tidy him up a bit. That way we get him to Romulus on schedule.' He raised an eyebrow. 'Yes?'

'Yes,' I said, not relishing the idea, finding no workable alternative.

We left GHQ at 04.50 hours, driving across the sleeping city, the houses shuttered, the streets deserted. Reynaud led in the jeep with two armed soldiers, I followed in the ambulance, four more soldiers in the back dressed as medical orderlies. The MPs guarding the house had been alerted and made a circle round the vehicles as we drew up, rifles cocked. Reynaud and I went in, up the dark stairs to the landing. The guard was there with a lantern. Reynaud told him to unlock the door and stood aside for me to enter.

Troax was sleeping peacefully. I touched his shoulder and put a finger to my lips as he opened his eyes. The last thing I wanted was for him to blurt out something about Johnson's visit. He nodded. 'Time to go, Michael?'

I said it was and he got up and pulled his cloak round himself, instantly wide-awake, eager to be off.

He stumbled as we started down the stairs. I held him up and he apologized. 'Legs a bit shaky. Sorry. It's the first time I've been out of that room for four years. I'll be all right in a minute.'

'I'll carry you down.'

'No need for that,' he said, the old independence sparking. 'I can manage.'

'I'll carry you,' I said. 'The last thing you want now is a broken leg.' I picked him up, shamed by the frailty of him. It was like carrying a twelve-year-old. He didn't weigh an ounce over six stone.

'You're the doctor,' he said.

The ambulance surprised him. 'What's this for?'

'Privacy.' I grinned, setting him on his feet. 'You don't want people to see you like this, in rags and tatters, do you? We're keeping you under wraps until we've got you smartened up for the court.'

He smiled his broken-toothed smile. 'VIP treatment, is it? No expense spared?'

'No more than you deserve if you're going to take the Senate by storm,' I said, the words like bile in my mouth.

'It's all fixed, then?'

'Day after tomorrow.'

'At last.' He sighed contentedly. 'And you'll be there?'

'Of course.'

'I'm glad. Thank you, Michael. For everything.'

I nodded, too ashamed to speak.

I saw him settled in the ambulance, immediately at ease with the medic soldiers in their white suits. Unsuspecting.

'You'll open the door only to me,' I said quietly to the senior man. 'Clear?'

'Sir.'

'Sponge him down and get him into clean clothes.' A blue-striped shirt, navy-blue suit, underwear, socks, shoes; all there ready in a wicker hamper. 'And go easy with him. He's had a bad time.'

The guard commander was waiting for me by the cab door, his head tilted back to look up at me under the peak of his red cap. 'Everything in order, sir?' he said, in the clipped voice of his trade. Military policemen were rumoured to make love to their wives by numbers.

'Thank you, Sar'nt. You know what to do now?'

'Sir. Stand by here till the coffin arrives.' With the substitute corpse to be carried upstairs and back down again for the benefit of passers-by. 'Then we lock up and leave.'

I nodded. 'If anyone asks, the prisoner died of a heart attack.'

'I'll see the word gets passed round, sir.' He hesitated. 'Glad it's not true, though. Plucky little cove, ain't he? He – he's going to be all right, is he, sir?'

'Oh, yes. He'll be fine.'

'Sir.' He saluted and stepped back.

I gave him some cash. 'Have a drink with the lads tonight. With my compliments.'

'Thank you very much, sir.' He saluted again, ramrod straight, all blanco and bright brass. But not without feelings.

I climbed up beside the driver. In the jeep, Reynaud raised his arm and we were on the move. Committed.

There was a lay-by outside the main gate of the Stella with an all-night mobile coffee stall. Reynaud called a halt a hundred yards short of it and walked back. 'Better we don't come in with you, sir. Never know who might be watching. We'll hang on here and pick you up as you leave.'

'That's the better part of two hours,' I said doubtfully.

'Not much traffic for a while yet. We'll have the bonnet open and a tool-kit spread out. Just for the look of the thing.'

'Right.'

Two minutes later we reversed into a vacant slot at the end of a line of ambulances in the parking area. I told the driver to stay put, got out and went round the back and climbed in. Troax was sitting on one of the bunks, stripped to the waist. One of the medics was lathering his face to shave him. There were two thermos flasks of coffee and some mugs on the pull-down table behind the cab.

'Like a wet, sir?' A medic filled a mug and gave it to me. He jerked his head at Troax. 'Have you seen his back?' he said quietly, angrily. 'Some vicious bastard's really worked him over.'

'A long time ago,' I said. 'In Philippi.'

'Yeah?' He shook his head. 'Bloody Greeks.'

I hid a smile, caught Troax's eye and was given a wink. He was on top of the world. A shrunken, scarred waif with a weal-ridged back, his ribs visible under the prison-pale skin, his bad eye weeping. Sitting there in borrowed trousers without a thing to call his own. And bubbling with excitement.

Will you ever forgive me for this day's work? I thought. And winked back.

I finished my coffee as the medic wiped his newly shaven face and helped him into the striped shirt. He stood up, tucking it into his waistband. 'How do I look?' he said, smiling.

'You'll do,' I said. In fact the change in him was dramatic. Just to be out of that garret prison, shaved and wearing clean clothes, had given him a certain panache, a kind of spry confidence.

'Fit to appear in court?'

'Undoubtedly.' If he had been going to court. I turned to the senior medic. 'A word with you.'

We stepped outside. 'You didn't hear that. About the court.'

'Court, sir? What court would that be?'

I smiled. 'Good man.'

The first streaks of the sunrise were lightening the sky. A fine morning, just a hint of frost in the air. Above and beyond the single-storey laboratories the hospital windows were still brightly lit, still blind to the outside world. But not for much longer.

'Any chance of some breakfast, sir?' the medic said. 'We could nip over to the staff canteen, bring something back for you and the prisoner.'

It was a risk, but a slight one. The canteen would be crowded with ambulance crews. Safety in numbers. I nodded. 'Take the driver with you. Don't be too long.'

I watched them walk away; four men in white suits, the driver in clean blue overalls. Good men, hand-picked, reliable.

'What's the hold-up, Michael?' Troax said, sitting on the bunk, eager to be away.

'No hold-up. Everything's going like a clock.'

He looked at me sharply. 'You're hiding something from me, aren't you?'

'Why would I do that?'

'I don't know. You tell *me*.'

I explained that we had moved him early for security reasons; were now laying down a false trail to keep him safe. 'You're an important prisoner, Paul. Nero's prisoner. It's my job to get you into the court in one piece.'

He smiled wryly. 'Good try, Michael, but I know you too well. We've always been honest with each other, haven't we? Trusted each other?'

I nodded miserably.

'So?' he asked.

'You're a bit worked-up. A prey to imagined fears. Natural enough in the circumstances. The first few hours of freedom can be traumatic.'

'Freedom? You call this freedom? You say I'm an important prisoner. But a prisoner just the same. So just tell me straight what's going on.'

Looking back I know I should never have let the medics go. In their presence it was possible to keep up the pretence, avoid awkward questions. But face to face with him, the two of us shut up in that ambulance, I knew the game was up. That I would have to tell him the truth.

When I did he was shocked. The colour drained out of his face, his shoulders slumped, all his confidence evaporated. 'I'm sorry, Paul. But it's out of my hands now.'

'It was never in them, was it?' he said bitterly. 'We're both pawns on some political chessboard.' He shook his head in despair. 'Exiled for life on some miserable little island. Spirited away without a chance to defend myself.' He sighed. 'I could've escaped, y'know. More than once. Peter's been at me for years to let him mount a rescue. Sent me plans through some of the women. And last night he came himself to try to persuade me.'

'I know. I've seen the guard commander's report. That's why we came early.'

'You needn't have bothered. I wouldn't let him try.' His good eye stared at me accusingly. 'If I'd known what was in store for me I might have. Better to be in hiding in Rome than out of touch on a lump of rock in the Aegean. I might as well be dead.'

I pointed out to him that the alternative was unthinkable. That if we let him go in front of Nero and the Senate not only would he die but hundreds of innocent people too. The whole Christian community in the city at the mercy of the mob. 'When they condemn you they'll condemn all those who trust and follow you.'

His head came up defiantly. '*If* they condemn me.'

I said levelly, 'When you say what you're going to say in court you'll condemn yourself as you did before Agrippa.' As Jesus Davidson had condemned himself before the Sanhedrin.

'You don't think they'll believe me?'

'Whether they believe you or not, Nero will have you killed. You're his scapegoat. His passport to staying alive and in control.'

'So it's all been in vain? My life of hardship and suffering. My little churches meeting in secret, filled with hope, true to the Faith. All just a waste. Is that what you're saying?'

'I'm saying you've done a magnificent job. Sown the seeds of a new religion which one day will command the attention – and the loyalty – of thousands of people. But that day has not yet come. When it does you'll be remembered as a great pioneer. The man who took a Jewish sect and made it a world Faith.'

He shrugged impatiently. 'I'm no hero, Michael, to be remembered with honour. I'm just a...'

'Stubborn little man who will be remembered – if at all – as the one whose pride brought misery and death to those who trusted him. A man determined to go down in a blaze of glory after his final confrontation with the State and never mind how many suffer for it. Is that what you want?'

'You know it's not,' he said, the hurt in his voice like a knife under my ribs.

I nodded. 'I know, Paul. Forgive me, but it had to be said.'

'Yes. But just to disappear without a word.' He sighed heavily. 'It's pathetic. A miserable anticlimax. Like a play with the last act missing.'

'It may not be for long,' I said. 'Nero's time is running out fast now and there are many good men in Rome making their plans, waiting for the chance to take over and start to repair the damage he's done.

'Public-spirited men of integrity and honour, faithful to the principles of their fathers. A couple of years, three at the most, and we could be sharing in the rebirth of the Empire. A constitution based on justice and decency and the freedom of the common people. We Christians could make a vital contribution to that. Give it the framework it will need. And you could come back a free man to take your place as our leader, your work vindicated, your faith rewarded.'

He shook his head. 'It'll be too late then. Exile in isolation will sap my strength. I'll be an old and withered has-been of no use to anyone. No, old friend. If I go now I'll not come back.'

I knew he was right. He'd psyched himself up to face Nero. That was all that was keeping him going. A thinker like John Zebedee could live alone on Patmos and write and dream and flourish, making a massive contribution to the Christian ethos. But Troax did his thinking on his feet; a crowd-puller needing opposition to bring out the best in him. Without an audience he was a spent force.

I said gently, 'Remember when we talked about John the Baptizer? How he stepped down at the height of his powers to give the Master the stage?'

'"He must increase and I must decrease."' He nodded. 'Yes, I remember.'

And the way he said it, the humility and despair behind the words, settled in my mind. Ferris was right. Troax had to go. But to an island, without a friend, without hope?

And I knew I couldn't let them do that to him.

2

We came out on to the Appian Way bang on schedule, the jeep's headlights blazing, our blue lamp flashing. The sun was well up now, white clouds like galleons sailing in from the sea. Semper, the driver, eased into fifth gear and put his foot down. What little traffic there was on our side of the dual carriageway pulled over to let us through, our speed mocking the slow queues of commuters' cars crawling into the city.

I sat beside Semper watching the half-mile marker posts springing up along the hard shoulder like the bars of a cage. Troax's cage closing in around him with every mile. My mind was racing, searching for a way to rescue him, discarding one wild idea after another, getting desperate.

Forty minutes later we turned off on to the slip road five miles from Romulus, came down to the roundabout and took the second exit into a narrow country road winding between hedges and tall rows of poplars. Too late now to formulate a workable plan. The aircraft would be fuelled outside the hangar, the crew standing by to receive us. I finally accepted the inevitability of this and decided to insist on flying with him to the airstrip at Syracuse – and transferring to the Transport Command workhorse laid on there for the onward flight to Piraeus if necessary – in the hope of helping him to make a break for it before he boarded the naval vessel for the last leg of his journey. I knew it was a vain hope but it was all I had left to work on.

The jeep was disappearing round a bend some sixty yards ahead when it happened.

A battered, high-sided, three-ton truck with a stained canvas tilt emerged without warning from a field gate and turned left to follow the jeep. Semper swore spectacularly, braked hard, flicked on the switch of the siren and dropped into first gear. The ambulance lurched and swerved. The tailgate of the truck rose like a wall in front of us, blocking our view.

'Bloody farmers,' Semper said savagely. 'No more road sense than a rabbit.'

'Can you squeeze past him?'

'Not a chance, sir.' He thumped the wheel in frustration. 'Of all the rotten luck!'

But was it luck or was it planned? A tiny spark of hope flickered in my mind. Had we been deliberately separated from the jeep? Reynaud would know nothing of the truck; be watching in his mirror for us to appear round the corner. How many more bends had he gone round since we last saw him? Surely he would hear the siren? There was only one answer to those questions.

As if reading my thoughts, the driver of the truck slewed it across the road and stopped.

'Damn the fool,' Semper growled. 'Now what?'

A movement in the mirror caught my eye. I saw a car turn out of the gate behind us and reverse down, boxing us in.

The tilt flaps on the three-tonner were pulled aside and half-a-dozen men in overalls and black knitted hats jumped down. In a moment we were surrounded. The men carried wooden clubs and looked only too eager to use them. Semper's door was wrenched open. A hand came in, cut the siren, switched off the engine and threw the keys away. As he did so, my door swung back and I was confronted by a big, heavily built man with a broken nose and bright, steady eyes. He was just as Troax had described him. Peter Johnson, sometime fisherman, reckless as ever, come to rescue his friend.

'Shalom,' he said. A peaceful greeting belied by the knife in his hand, its point pricking my neck.

I sat very still, meeting his eyes, holding them. Troax had told me of this man's hair-trigger temper, of his usefulness with a knife. 'A good friend, Michael,' he had said. 'And a formidable enemy.' The only one of the original Twelve who had fought to save Davidson from his captors the night before he died.

'How many in the back, Colonel?' he said pleasantly. He had a deep, Hebraic voice, round and full and ribbed with steel.

I hesitated.

'Don't play games with me, mate.' The pressure on the knife increased. 'I haven't the time and I'm not in the mood.'

'Four medics and the prisoner.' I felt the ambulance rock as the back doors were opened.

Johnson raised his voice. 'You men in there. Let Paul Troax step out nice and easy. No tricks. I'm holding a knife to the colonel's throat. Don't make me use it by doing something stupid.' He gave me a hard smile. 'I will if I have to.'

I called, 'Do as he says. I'll take full responsibility.' And added quietly, 'I wondered when you'd come, Johnson.'

His eyes flickered, surprised. 'You know my name?'

'Of course.' I smiled. 'I'm Michael Lucas. I'm on your side in this.'

He nodded. 'I've heard of you.' He looked past me at Semper sitting hunched over the wheel. 'You. Out. Now.'

He stepped back. 'You too, Colonel, if you please.'

He gripped my wrist as I stepped down, twisting my arm up behind my back. The point of the knife was cold on the back of my neck. 'Easy now. If you're who you say you are you've nothing to fear from me.'

We walked round to the back of the ambulance. Semper was inside with the medics, two of Johnson's men tying them up with lengths of cord. Troax was standing in the road, spruce in his borrowed suit. He saw the knife in Johnson's hand. 'No need for that, Peter. He's a friend.' He smiled at me. 'Sorry about this, Michael, but I really don't like islands.' He didn't look in the least sorry. He was back on form, full of life, jaunty. Free for the first time in four years and revelling in it.

I said, 'It won't work, y'know, Paul.'

He shrugged. 'We'll see. Worth a try, though, don't you think?'

Johnson released me, sheathing his knife. His men climbed down, slammed the ambulance doors and locked them. Beyond the truck I heard the squeal of brakes, the jeep's horn blaring.

'Time to go, boys,' Johnson said. And shouted, 'Light the fire, Jake.'

The man standing beside the truck opened the cab door and took out a bottle with a strip of cloth stuffed into the neck. He lit it, ran round to the rear and tossed it inside. I heard the sound of breaking glass and saw a great tongue of flame shoot up through the tilt.

Troax and I were bundled into the back of the car. Johnson slid in beside the driver. His men were stripping off their overalls and woollen hats and throwing them into the boot. Underneath, they were wearing the flannel shirts and jeans of farm labourers. They slammed down the boot lid, ran through the gate and disappeared into the trees.

'When you're ready, Steedie,' Johnson said equably.

I looked through the rear window as we accelerated away. The truck was blazing fiercely; a barrier of fire Reynaud couldn't hope to get past.

'All right, Colonel?' Johnson said.

'My name's Mike.'

'Mike it is then.' He thrust his arm over the seat back and shook my hand. 'Welcome to our community, Mike.'

I grinned. 'Shalom, Peter.'

'Oh yes. You'll do. The Master would approve of you. He always had a soft spot for the military. Men under authority, see? As we all are, of course. The authority of God.' It was said matter-of-factly but with enormous sincerity.

And I'm in the presence of his high command, I thought; the little Roman Jew and the big street-fighter.

The morning rush hour was over when we turned on to the Appian Way. The car went over the tarmac like a hot iron over a sheet, cruising comfortably at eighty. It was an old Hermes GT8 saloon with the distinctive long bonnet and big chrome headlights of the marque. The paintwork was scored and dented, the seats sagging under us, but the big eight-cylinder engine fed by twin carburettors ran sweet and smooth, purring with silky strength. A driver's car and Steedie could drive it. He was a young Greek with the open face of a schoolboy and red-brown curly hair. And he knew how to handle a car.

'Where are we going, Peter?' Troax said, unperturbed, enjoying himself.

'The catacombs. Where else?'

The catacombs were caves deep underground in waste land outside the city, originally excavated by the Jews to bury their dead when the municipal cemeteries were barred to them.

Troax saw my puzzlement. 'We took them over some time back, Michael, to shelter our people from the police.'

'You mean people are actually living there?' I said.

Johnson grinned. 'Surprising what you can get used to if you have to.'

'Yes. I suppose so,' I said doubtfully.

'How did you get on to us, Peter?' Troax said.

'Jake,' Johnson said. 'The man who fired the truck. His sister works in GHQ as a clerk. A pretty face and a quick mind. She keeps us informed about you. At some personal risk, you understand? She rang me early this morning before she came off duty.' He smiled. 'We did a good job, eh? No casualties on either side.'

But the medics and Semper would have some explaining to do. Five armed men taken with the point of a knife. And Reynaud would get a rocket from Ferris.

'Awkward for you, though, Michael,' Troax said.

I shrugged. 'I just went along for the ride. I'm retired, remember?' I would have to write a report, of course. The inevitable paper-work. To be filed away and forgotten.

We drove in silence for a mile or two, the buildings in the city rising ahead of us now, tall and white in the morning sun. The Greek in me insisted it was not to be compared with Athens. Strength without beauty, weight without grace. But it was the heart of the Empire and would need more than a band of amateur guerrillas to topple it. 'How far are you taking me?' I said then.

'There's a hotel a mile or so this side of the city boundary,' Johnson said. 'We'll drop you off there. Leave you to sit on the terrace with a flask of wine. The way *we* used to do with the Master in the good days when it was all going his way.' He grinned. 'The rabbis didn't like it, of course. Put it about that he was a drop-out and a wino. Any stick to beat him with, y'see. But we knew he was God's own son come down to share our troubles – and our pleasures. "Be kind to your stomachs, lads," he used to say. "A little wine works wonders for the digestion."'

I looked at Troax. 'I thought *you* said that?'

'I was quoting him, Michael. All my best speeches were borrowed from him.'

I heard the wistfulness in his voice and wondered if this was part of the penance he had set himself; to quote the words of the man he had once hated, whose followers he had hunted down without mercy. The longer I knew him, the more complex he became. And the more admirable. Behind the forceful street orator, skilled with words, was a man of deep humility haunted by guilt, closer to the Master he had never seen than even Peter Johnson.

'Give us half an hour to disappear before you phone for transport, eh?' Johnson said.

I hesitated. 'I'm not happy about you going into the catacombs. It's the first place they'll think of looking for you.' And the last place Troax needed after four years in that garret. Buried alive in an underground cave like a rabbit cowering from the ferrets. What would that do to

his mind, his restless, eager spirit? 'I think you should
drop Paul off with me at the hotel.'

Johnson's head came round. 'You're not serious?'

'Look,' I said. 'Nobody knows what he looks like.
Nobody but his guards has seen him for years. I'll take
him as my patient.'

'Where to, Michael? Where will we go?'

'Tremezzo. To my place. Off the map. Out of sight.
Safe.' I smiled at him. 'A few months up there. Good
food, good air, plenty of healthy exercise. A long way
from prying eyes in Rome. Get you back on your feet
for...'

'For what?'

'That's up to you, Paul. You'll be my guest, not my
prisoner. A free man again. Sit tight and make your plans
until things have settled down. Nero can't last much
longer. And when he goes – who knows what
opportunities you may have to further the Faith?'

Johnson shook his head. 'I don't know. Sounds a bit
risky to me.'

'Not as risky as the catacombs,' I said. 'Or as
frustrating.'

Troax nodded. 'Michael's right, Peter. I've had my fill
of prisons.'

'What'll you tell your man in GHQ?' Johnson said.

'That Paul's dead. Struck down in that ambush in the
lane. His body thrown into the burning truck. I shall
get a severe reprimand, of course. Just to save a few
faces.'

'And while you're explaining yourself, what'll Paul be
doing?'

'Paul will be on the train for Milan, the key of my
house in his pocket.'

'Hmm. It might work at that,' Johnson said reluctantly. 'All right. We drop you at the hotel. Both of you.'

But we never got that far.

3

'Now what?' Johnson said harshly, leaning forward to peer through the windscreen.

We had just topped a long rise and the road ahead was laid out like a map below us. Down there a police van was parked across the outside lane, its blue lamp rotating. A line of cones was angled to funnel traffic on to the hard shoulder where a barrier of stout white poles barred the way.

'Accident?' Troax said, his voice suddenly tired, brittle with tension. He had emerged from the cocoon of the garret into a big, violent world of excitement and danger and fragile hope. A world he had once known and thrived in but to which he was now a stranger.

'No wreckage. No ambulance.' Johnson was thinking aloud. 'Spot check on faulty vehicles. Has to be.'

'Unless they're on to us,' Steedie said tightly, voicing all our fears.

'No way. Those boys in the jeep'll still be trapped in that lane.'

Or in touch with GHQ from the guard room in Romulus. Piers Reynaud was not one to stand and watch a truck burn out.

'Ease up a bit, Steedie. We'll bluff our way through.'

'And me in uniform?' I said. 'No chance.'

'We picked you up back there. Your car broke down. You needed a lift.' Johnson gave me a fierce grin. 'Like you said, nobody knows what Paul looks like.'

We slid past the police van at a prudent 20 mph, following the line of cones. A mobile radio truck was parked just before the barrier, a police sergeant standing outside it. He was wearing a flak jacket and carrying a revolver on his hip. He flagged us down, bent to look into the car and saluted me. 'Morning, Colonel. Sorry to bother you.'

'Is there a problem?' I said.

He looked at Troax and then at Johnson. 'Who are these men, sir?'

I told him Johnson's story.

'I see, sir.' His voice was carefully neutral. 'So you don't know anything about these men?'

'Only that they've gone out of their way to help me.'

'Yes.' He opened the door. 'If you wouldn't mind stepping out for a moment, sir?' he said politely. The daunting politeness of his kind, brooking no argument. He had an intelligent face and speculative eyes and he had done this sort of thing many times.

I got out and closed the door. 'Well?'

'Am I right in thinking you're Colonel Lucas, sir?'

So it was all for my benefit; the blocked carriageway, the cones, the barrier. Reynaud had been busy. 'Yes, I'm Lucas. Why?'

'We'll talk in the truck, sir, if you please.'

The radio operator sitting at the console turned his head as we entered.

'Have you been hurt, sir?' the sergeant said.

'No.'

'Only there's blood on your collar.'

I shrugged. 'I nicked myself shaving.'

The sergeant gave me an unbelieving smile. 'Of course.' He nodded to the operator. 'Patch us through to the Brigadier.'

The operator dialled a number and handed me a

head-set. There was a crackle of static in my ear and then the familiar, rasping voice. 'Ferris.'

'Lucas here, sir.'

'Ah, Mike. I wondered when you'd turn up. Are you all right?'

'Yes.' I jerked my head at the sergeant. He and the operator went outside.

'So?' Ferris said impatiently.

I filled him in on what had happened. The ambush in the lane, the torched truck, the men who had bundled me into the car and dumped me on the Appian Way. The passing motorist who had given me a lift.

He grunted. 'Any casualties?'

'Only one, sir. Troax.'

'Badly hurt?'

'He's dead, I'm afraid. Shot in the head. His body thrown into the burning truck.' The lies came smoothly, being in a good cause.

'You saw it?'

'Yes. There was a knife at my throat at the time.'

'Uncomfortable. Who were they, these men? D'you know?'

'My guess is that they're Jewish insurgents settling an old score with an apostate.'

'Ghetto rats, eh?' Ferris growled. 'Makes sense, I suppose. They've been after him for years.' And that, at least, was true. Ever since Damascus, from Israel through Turkey and Greece, the orthodox Jews had been Troax's worst enemies, gunning for him in every city, every town. 'So that's it, then.' I heard the relief in his voice, the problem finally solved, his hands clean. 'And you're sure you're all right, Mike?'

'Well enough. I'm getting too old for this game.'

He chuckled. 'Well, the game's over now. I'll send a car to bring you in. A celebratory dinner tonight, I think. And back to Tremezzo tomorrow. Yes?'

Before I could answer there was a sudden commotion outside. Shouted orders, a car engine starting up, the squeal of tyres. I dropped the head-set, whipped open the door and jumped down.

Armed police, hidden behind the truck until now, were fanning out in an arc across the tarmac. Ahead of them the old Hermes on full throttle rammed into the barrier. Splintered poles were tossed into the air to smash down on the long bonnet. The police opened fire as it broke through, swerving wildly, the engine howling. The near-side rear tyre took a bullet and blew out. The car zigzagged out of control, Steedie wrestling with the wheel. The suspension collapsed under the strain and it rolled over and slid to a halt on its side. The engine stalled.

The sergeant shouted, 'Hold your fire.'

I ran through the line of policemen and saw the front passenger door pushed up like a hatch and Johnson climbing out, his face running with blood from a gash to his forehead. He dropped down to face me, his knife in his hand, his eyes blazing.

I stopped in my tracks, shielding him from the marksmen. 'Peter, for God's sake. There's no need for this.'

He glared at me, hyped-up, uncertain, dangerous.

'It was all buttoned up as I promised.' The loose ends neatly tied, Ferris satisfied. 'We could've driven away as we planned.'

His eyes flickered. The hand holding the knife dropped to his side. 'Sorry, Mike,' he said hoarsely, the victim of his own impetuosity. 'We thought – I thought you'd got on the radio and...'

'Betrayed you?'

He shook his head. 'I'm sorry. I...' He turned abruptly and ran round the front of the car.

'No. Wait,' I shouted.

But if he heard me he took no notice.

I watched in despair as he leaped over the guard rail on the central reservation and went dodging and jinking through the traffic on the far side. Horns blared at him. Cars swerved crazily to avoid him. A coach full of children missed him by inches. Incredibly, impossibly, he got across, charged up a steep grassy bank, stood for a moment on the crest tall against the sky, raised an arm in farewell and was gone.

Unable to use their weapons for fear of hitting the drivers in the stream of traffic, the police stood in stunned disbelief.

Oh, Peter Johnson, I thought. Big, brash Peter. It's the catacombs for you now. They're on to you and will hunt you down, however long it takes.

And I knew it would not be long. A free spirit like his was not made to hide away among the dead. Two weeks, three at the most, and he would be out again, taking command, rallying the Christian community, inviting trouble.

I climbed up on to the Hermes and looked inside. The car stank of petrol and the sickly smell of blood. Steedie was beyond help, a spoke from the broken steering wheel protruding from his chest, his matted hair slicked with blood. In the rear seat Troax was wedged against the door, his eyes closed, his face unmarked and strangely peaceful. He appeared to be uninjured but when I reached in and touched him his head fell limply to one side and I knew his neck was broken.

I should have realized Johnson would never have left him had he been alive.

Standing below me, the sergeant said, 'Dead?'

I nodded and got down stiffly.

'Both of them?'

'Yes.' The muscles in my legs were trembling as reaction set in and I leaned against the wrecked Hermes, appalled by the irony of it all. To come through so much – ridicule, physical abuse, mental strain; the endless journeys, the prison cells, the shipwreck – only to die like this, uselessly, without cause. Was this the reward of faith?

The sergeant cleared his throat. 'The little fellow, sir. Was he a friend of yours?'

'Yes. I'm proud to say he was.'

'Ah,' he said, aware of my grief, puzzled by it. 'I'm sorry. Very sorry.'

'Yes. Thank you.'

It was a day for being sorry.

4

'I thought you said he'd been shot, his body burned in the truck?' Ferris said accusingly. 'And now you're telling me he was killed in a car crash?'

It was one o'clock in the afternoon and we were having a working lunch in his office. Cheese and pickle sandwiches, a tall jug of beer.

I shrugged. 'The result's the same, sir. Troax is dead. He'll not trouble you again.'

'Just an anonymous corpse in the prison morgue?'

'Yes.' He and Steedie side by side, white-sheeted on the cold slabs under the fluorescent lights.

'That police sergeant. He doesn't know who he is?'

'Not a clue.' A sight of my CI2 card had been enough to ensure his co-operation, stifle his questions.

'No loose ends waiting to trip us up?'

'No. Nothing.' I saw the relief on his face, took a deep breath and said, 'I want to take him home, sir. Give him a decent burial on my property.' Instead of an unmarked grave in the prison cemetery. 'A private affair. No fuss, no priest, no mourners.'

He raised suspicious eyebrows. 'Why?'

'Personal reasons, sir.'

He gave me a long stare. 'He meant that much to you?'

I nodded.

'Hmm. You're pushing your luck, Lucas.'

'Sir.'

'You understand that if anything goes wrong and the media get wind of it you'll be on your own? I shall disown all knowledge of him. And of you.'

'Of course. My responsibility.'

'You never worked for me. All your reports will be shredded, all connections with this office denied.'

'I understand.' He was not one to leave his tracks uncovered.

'You'll have to make all the arrangements yourself, without official backing.'

'I've already done that.' A wad of cash folded into the morgue attendant's hand had smoothed the way.

'Have you, by God?' Ferris chuckled. 'Damned impudence. Still it's as good a way as any to close the file, I suppose. Better than the lions, eh?'

'Or the living death of exile.'

'Oh, that was never on the cards, Mike. Too risky by half. I doubt there's an island remote enough to have kept that little firebrand out of trouble.'

'But I thought...'

'What you were meant to think.'

'But it was all laid on from Romulus through Syracuse to Greece and...'

'To Syracuse, yes. No further than that. We had a medic on the plane to inoculate him. Typhus, tetanus, yellow fever. The usual cocktail. Plus one more.'

I looked at him, shaken. 'You mean...?'

'A quick and easy death, Mike, one that any one of us would opt for given the choice.' He shook his head. 'I'm sorry, but it had to be done.'

'I could've done that for him.'

'But you wouldn't, would you?'

'No,' I said dully, remembering that moment in the attic when...

'Have some more beer.' He filled my glass from the jug. 'And don't look so affronted. You know the way the

Firm works.' He grinned. 'When you come to think about it, not many dead men leave three corpses. One in the morgue to satisfy Nero. One incinerated in a truck. One you're taking home to Tremezzo. Remarkable.'

'Yes.' It was the sort of bizarre situation Troax would have appreciated. 'He was a remarkable man, sir.'

Ferris nodded. 'I suppose he was. Pity he changed sides back there in Damascus. If he'd stayed in Caiaphas' camp he'd have been no threat to us. An educated, orthodox Jew with Roman citizenship. Our man in Jerusalem, in fact, ideally placed to maintain the balance between Church and State.' He shrugged. 'All thrown away for the sake of a Galilean carpenter who thought he was God.'

'He was never a threat to us,' I said flatly.

Ferris raised his eyebrows. 'How can you say that? You've seen him in action, read his subversive letters to his followers. Every report you've filed is evidence that he was plotting a revolution to bring the Empire down. Establishing bases in city after city, country after country. Every word he spoke a call to arms.'

'No,' I said. 'That's what we thought – how it looked. But he wasn't a revolutionary. He was a reformer. He knew the Empire is crumbling as all empires crumble. Riddled with corruption. Destroying itself. Vulnerable to its enemies. What he was doing was building an alternative Kingdom to replace it when the time comes. An international Kingdom of peace and justice whose King is God himself.'

'Wasting his time, then, wasn't he?' Ferris said, 'As Jesus Davidson did.'

'That remains to be seen, sir,' I said.

EPILOGUE

The mason in Menaggio brought the headstone this morning; a finely chiselled tablet of white marble with PAULUS cut into it in plain letters. It seemed appropriate to use the Latin form of his name. He had been so proud to be a Roman.

Just the name. No dates, no inscription. I had toyed with the idea of having an ichthus – the Christian fish symbol – carved on the stone. Or IHS. *Iesus Hominum Salvator.* But I decided against it. Nero's spies are everywhere – even in Como. No point in inviting trouble.

It's just ten days since he died. I still find it hard to believe; expect to meet him on the road by the lake, swinging along with that tireless, jaunty lope of his, seeking the excitement he craved. Every time the phone rings I think it will be him, full of plans to strike out into France and Spain. Only natural, I suppose. We were together in so many crises. He once called me his guardian angel. I was never that. Just an informer who became a friend.

I dug a grave for him on the crest of a little hill at the top of my garden beside a Lombardy poplar. A tree as tall and as noble as the spirit crammed into that worn, misshapen body. It's a pleasant spot sheltered by the mountains, commanding a magnificent view up the lake to the Alps. Where I intend to lie when my time comes.

The body came up on the Como train in a plain, pine coffin. I rented a station wagon and brought him back to the house. The coffin was surprisingly light. I tied two lengths of rope to the tree and was able to lower it easily into the grave. I filled it in and stood alone in the sunlight.

I have never been to a Christian funeral, have no idea what their burial rites are. But I know that for them death is only a step from darkness into light, as Jesus Davidson proved by his resurrection more than thirty years ago. I find it oddly reassuring that Paul, like his Master, had taken that liberating step in April – the month of new life.

And suddenly he was there in the garden with me. No longer a vagrant from the Tarsus ghetto, ugly, reviled, burning with the anger of love, but a universal man – Jew, Roman, Christian – who had won the affection and gratitude of thousands of men and women whose lives he had transformed. They, not this headstone, were his true memorial.

So I said a Paternoster for him. For us both. The prayer of the Master which encapsulates every prayer. Still, for me, a prayer of wistful hope. But for him a triumphant statement of fact. 'For thine is the Kingdom...'

And I said, 'Shalom, old friend. Peace be with you.' And walked back alone down the hill.

There's a full moon tonight rising in splendour over the mountains across the lake. From my window I can see the little white stone by the tree reflecting its serenity. And, at the foot of the stone, a bunch of flowers.

They had not been there before supper. One of the village women had put them there, I suppose. Somebody who had seen the mason bringing the headstone this morning. A gesture of sympathy for me, the newcomer who has buried a friend? Probably. Country folk are like that, doing in secret under the cover of darkness what they are too shy to do publicly.

Or is it perhaps more than that?

Peter Johnson will have spread the news of Paul's death among the Christians in Rome and news of that kind travels fast and far by word of mouth. Could it be that there is already a Christian church in Como? Or even here in Tremezzo?

That the flowers on his grave are a gesture not only of sympathy but also of faith?

Also by Lion Publishing

The Davidson Affair

Stuart Jackman

Executed for treason on Friday, Davidson is rumoured to be alive again on Sunday.

Cass Tennel is despatched to Jerusalem to report for the Imperial Television Corporation. He has thirty-six hours to investigate the truth about Davidson before going live to the Roman empire in a documentary on Monday evening. But what is the truth and what should he make of the many interviews he conducts? From Governor-General Pilate to the infamous belly dancer Mary Magdala, everyone he talks to has a different story to tell, or to hide.

This remarkably original and highly readable novel explores the motives and fears of the main characters in the gospel stories, translating them into familiar situations and common speech with supreme confidence.

ISBN 0 7459 3973 2